AN UNDERWATER ENCOUNTER

Something was coming out, racing toward them through the water in a cloud of silt and sand.

Something huge.

"Look out!" yelled Jessie.

"Holy hopping admirals!" cried Race Bannon, who was standing behind Jonny and Jessie, looking over their shoulders at the monitor.

Emerging from the racing cloud was a tentacle as big around as a tree trunk.

It was followed by another, and another.

And then by a wriggling mass, in the center of which was a sharp beak, opening and closing.

"A *gianter* giant squid!" Jonny said.

"It's the *mama* squid!" breathed Jessie.

"It's XZXZXZXXZXZXZXZX fast," said Dr. Quest on the speakerphone through static. "Pull us up! Quick!"

Read all of
The Real Adventures of Jonny Quest™
books

The Demon of the Deep
The Forbidden City of Luxor
The Pirates of Cyber Island*

by Brad Quentin

*coming soon

THE DEMON
OF THE DEEP

BRAD QUENTIN

HarperPrism

An Imprint of HarperPaperbacks

This is a work of fiction. The characters, incidents, and
dialogues are products of the author's imagination and are not to
be construed as real. Any resemblance to actual events or persons,
living or dead, is entirely coincidental.

HarperPaperbacks *A Division of* HarperCollins*Publishers*
10 East 53rd Street, New York, N.Y. 10022

First printing: August 1996

Printed in the United States of America

HarperPaperbacks, HarperPrism and colophon are trademarks of
HarperCollins*Publishers*

❖ 10 9 8 7 6 5 4 3 2 1

THE DEMON OF THE DEEP

1

"THERE IT IS!" SAID HADJI.

He pointed over the side of the boat, into the deep green rushing water.

Jonny Quest leaned out and peered over the rail.

"It's huge!" he agreed.

He saw a great dark triangle, almost as large as the Quest catamaran itself, following the sailboat's twin wake as it sliced through the shimmering waters of the South Pacific.

It looked like a shadow, except that its huge wings flapped slowly in the dark water.

"But it doesn't have any tentacles," said Jonny, a little disappointed. "The thing we're supposed to be looking for has ten."

"Even better," Hadji said. "Maybe this is some kind of totally unknown sea monster. An all-new undiscovered demon of the deep!"

"Not exactly," said a deep voice behind them.

The boys looked up and saw Race Bannon, one of the two adult leaders of the Quest Team, standing over them, his massive shoulders blocking out the sun.

"What you see below the boat, following us, is a giant ray," said Race. "They are awesome, I agree, but not particularly rare. They often follow boats in this area. Some of the New Zealand fishermen even think they bring good luck."

"So it's not a monster?" asked Hadji.

"Not a demon of the deep?" Jonny grinned.

"Hardly," said Race Bannon, his steely features screwing into a grin. The former Navy SEAL rarely smiled, but when he did, it was like the sun breaking through clouds.

"Though there may be a real monster close by," said another voice.

It was the world-famous scientist, Doctor Benton Quest, Jonny's dad and the leader of the Quest Team. With him was Jessie Bannon, Race's teenage daughter, the best friend and companion of Jonny and Hadji.

"Where?" said Jessie and Hadji, both running to the rail and peering back into the water.

Jonny knew better. He could tell by his father's tone that Dr. Quest was in what Jonny called his "lecture mode."

"If you want to see the real sea monster, look for your reflection in the water," said Dr. Quest. "We humans are the ones that foul the air and pollute the seas. We spoil the seven seas with bloody wars, and we kill our animal brothers and sisters with oil spills and pollution."

"Woof," said Bandit, Jonny's dog, the smallest member of the Quest Team, running from his usual station at the bow—or front—of the boat.

"What makes a *monster* is a question of point of view," Dr. Quest continued. "We humans are the only creatures that make war on our own kind and destroy the environment."

"I agree," said Hadji, whose practice of yoga had taught him respect for all life.

"But hold on, there, Benton" said Race Bannon, who thought his boss's views were a little too extreme. "We humans aren't *all* bad. We are also the only life form that tries to save the planet and protect endangered species."

"That's right, Dad," said Jessie, eager to enter the debate. "After we endanger them in the first place!"

"You both have a point," said Dr. Quest. "But we'll have to continue the debate later. We are nearing our destination, and I came back here to call you all together."

Dr. Quest pointed toward the center of the catamaran, where a video monitor had been set up on the control board at the base of the mast.

"Let's gather at the center of the boat for a briefing on our mission!"

"Woof," said Bandit, scurrying forward.

While Jessie and Hadji followed Race Bannon and

3

Dr. Quest forward for the briefing, Jonny paused and looked again over the railing at the stern of the boat.

The giant ray was still there, following the Quest catamaran like a shadow.

"We are in the South Pacific, as you all know, on a special mission," said Dr. Benton Quest.

Jonny, Hadji, and Jessie were sitting cross-legged on the deck. Race Bannon, who was Dr. Quest's bodyguard as well as his colleague, stood by the mast, poised for action even though there was no danger. Vigilance was a constant habit for Race Bannon, a habit formed by his years as a special "op" with the Agency and as a Navy SEAL.

"One of the most mysterious and wonderful creatures on earth is the giant squid," Dr. Quest continued. "It is known to us only through legend."

Dr. Quest clicked his remote and the monitor showed an illustration from a CD-ROM encyclopedia—an old engraving of a sailing ship being dragged underwater by giant tentacles, while screaming men jumped overboard.

"Ugh!" said Hadji.

"Woof!" said Bandit.

"Cool!" said Jessie.

"That's just a drawing!!" protested Jonny. "Aren't there any photos?"

4

"The giant squid lives so deep under the ocean that it has never been observed in its natural habitat. Only a few sightings have occurred, on the rare occasions when the great beast has risen to the surface. None of these have been in modern times."

"That means if we get a video, we'll be the first," said Hadji.

"Precisely," said Dr. Quest.

"How do we know it's for real?" asked Jonny. "What if it's just a myth, like the dragon or the unicorn?"

"The unicorn is NOT a myth," Jessie whispered fiercely. Her greatest wish was to find the unicorn, which she was convinced really existed.

Dr. Quest clicked the remote again, and the monitor screen showed a black-and-white photo of a man standing beside something that looked like a deflated weather balloon.

"Here is a giant squid that was pulled up in a net off the coast of New Zealand last year. Unfortunately, it was already dead by the time this picture was taken."

"How big was it?" Hadji asked.

"Forty feet long, including the tentacles," said Dr. Quest.

"Seems pretty big to me," said Bannon.

"Actually it is the largest male ever found. The males are smaller than the females," said Dr. Benton Quest.

"So there!" whispered Jessie, the only female on the Quest Team. "How big do the females get?" she asked.

"That's anybody's guess," said Dr. Quest. "And that's one of the things we are here to discover. They may grow as big as seventy feet—twice the size of this male."

"The one in the old picture was bigger than that," said Bannon. "Big enough to pull a ship under!"

"We must allow for the exaggerations of legend," said Dr. Quest. "I would be very surprised if we were to come across an actual creature that huge!"

Jonny looked around the deck of the Quest catamaran. The ocean-going sailing vessel seemed nowhere near big enough for the beast Dr. Quest was describing.

"What are we going to catch the giant squid with?" Jonny asked. "And if we catch it, where are we going to keep it?"

Dr. Quest held up a video camera. "We're going to catch him with this," he said.

With his other hand, he held up a CD. "And we're going to keep him in here!"

"You mean *her*," Jessie whispered.

While Dr. Quest explained the mission, the Quest catamaran plunged smoothly through the ocean swells untended by human hands.

Designed and built by Dr. Quest, with Race Bannon's expert naval advice, the catamaran was one of the fastest and most versatile boats in the world—and one of the most energy-efficient.

Its sleek twin-hull design allowed it to streak through the water effortlessly, with rarely any need to fire up the auxiliary Wankel engine.

The highly efficient polymer sails caught every gust of wind, propelling the fiberglass hulls through the heaviest seas faster than a powerboat—and more comfortably, since the catamaran didn't roll with the waves as much as a conventional boat.

The sixty-foot vessel was held on course by a computer-controlled system that raised and lowered the sails, trimmed the rudder, and adjusted the centerboard automatically, responding to winds and currents and sailing the boat as surely and confidently as the autopilot flies a giant Boeing 777.

"With luck, we will be the first to video the creature in its lair," finished Dr. Quest. He rose to his feet and cracked his knuckles impatiently. His trim beard was wet with spray. As always, he was sucking on an unlit pipe. "Jessie, can you confirm our position?"

Jessie leaped to her feet and turned on the liquid crystal display on the catamaran's computer control board.

The display was linked to a positional satellite in high earth orbit, so that with the press of a button the navigators of the Quest catamaran could determine their exact position at any time, day or night.

"Latitude 43 degrees, 32 minutes; longitude 181 degrees, 11 minutes," Jessie read.

"Good," said Dr. Quest. "We are nearing our destination."

We are? thought Jonny. He looked on all sides, but all he could see was the trackless blue of the ocean.

"Hadji, Jonny, climb the mast to the crow's nest," Dr. Quest said.

"Aye, aye, sir!" both teens replied in unison.

They leaped to the ropes and scrambled up the mast. The crow's nest was a small platform ninety feet up. The height exaggerated the swaying of the mast; the crow's nest swooped out over the water as the catamaran rode the waves. It was almost like a carnival ride.

But Jonny and Hadji held on and scanned the horizon fearlessly.

"See anything?" Race Bannon called up.

"The water is changing color," Hadji called down. "It's deep green behind us, and a lighter green up ahead."

"Good," said Dr. Quest. "Bring her about, Race!"

Race Bannon spun the wheel and turned the sleek catamaran into the wind. The sails fluttered and the boat glided to a stop.

"Drop anchor!" called out Dr. Quest.

Jessie pressed a button connected to a hydraulic servo; there was a splash as the half-ton anchor hit the water and a whine as the cables ran down toward the sea bottom.

Jonny and Hadji climbed back down the mast. "You said we are near our destination," Jonny said. "But there's no land in sight."

"Our destination is straight below, over half a mile," said Dr. Quest, pointing down toward the deck. "We are over the southern edge of Chatham Rise, an undersea plateau a few hundred miles off the coast of New Zealand. The top of the plateau is almost a thousand feet below us. If my theory is correct, the cliffs and ravines that edge the plateau are where we will find *Architeuthis.*"

"Toothless?" asked Jessie, giggling. "We're looking for Toothless?"

"*Architeuthis,*" said Dr. Quest. "Rhymes with toothless. It's the scientific name for our quarry."

"The giant squid," said Jonny.

"The demon of the deep!" whispered Hadji.

"What makes you think this is the spot?" asked Jonny.

"Remember the photo we saw of the dead male? It was taken on a fishing boat near this very spot. For some reason, fishermen have caught several in the past year. Perhaps the increased fishing is disturbing them, causing them to come closer to the surface. If this is true, we will recommend that the fishing grounds be moved."

"We don't want to disturb them," said Hadji.

All the members of the Quest Team nodded in agreement. It was one of their principles, that all creatures had an equal right to live on the planet. Animals and plants as well as humans.

"Does Old Toothless have any teeth?" asked Jessie.

Dr. Quest shook his head. "No, but it has a beak as big as a shovel. The creature is not only toothless, but boneless. It is the planet's largest invertebrate."

"Invertebrate?" asked Hadji.

"*In* meaning *without*, *vertebrate* meaning *backbone*," said Dr. Quest. "We humans are vertebrates, animals with backbones—so are bears, and dogs, and snakes, and even the whales that feed on the giant squid. But the squid, like jellyfish or crabs, has no spine."

"A spineless creature," said Jonny Quest.

"Spineless perhaps, but not cowardly," said Dr. Quest. "As we will no doubt discover. But it is almost evening. Let's prepare dinner and get some rest. Our journey across the sea is over. Tomorrow our journey underneath it will begin."

That evening, after a dinner of freshly caught fish, Jonny sat with his two best friends at the bow.

10

The three teens leaned back and looked up at the stars, basking in the warm night air. "Hard to believe it's January," Jessie said.

When they had left the United States, the Quest compound had been covered with ice and snow. But here in the southern hemisphere, the seasons were reversed, and January was midsummer.

"How do you feel?" Jonny asked Hadji. "Scared?"

Hadji shrugged. Tomorrow he would be making the dive with Dr. Quest. Since Dr. Quest adopted him, Hadji Bingh had always shared equally in the dangers and rewards of the Quest Team.

"Of course, I'm scared," said Hadji. "Scared but excited, too."

Jonny envied his friend and brother's ability to admit his fear. Often Jonny was so pumped up on adrenaline that he didn't know if he was afraid or not.

"I'd be scared, too," Jessie said. "And you would be, too, Jonny Quest."

"We'll all get to make a dive sooner or later," said Hadji. "Meanwhile, there'll be plenty to do up here."

"While you are practicing your video skills!" said Jonny.

"Right on! Capturing the world's biggest what-do-you-call-it on video," said Hadji.

"Invertebrate," said Jessie. "In-ver-te-brate."

"Whatever," said Jonny and Hadji together.

"Ten bells," called out Race Bannon. The teens

looked at one another and grinned sleepily. Time for bed.

Jonny climbed into his bunk, as usual, with a book. Tonight it was *Moby Dick*.

Jonny Quest fell asleep and dreamed of the one-legged captain fighting the giant whale as it dragged his ship under the waves.

2

WHEN JONNY AWOKE, IT WAS MORNING. HE LOOKED AROUND and saw that the other bunks were empty. He could hear footsteps and voices on the deck above.

He tumbled out of his bunk into the small galley, lit by a skylight. He grabbed a poppy-seed bagel from the leftovers on the table, and went up on deck.

It was a beautiful bright clear day. A vapor trail high overhead showed where a passenger jet was passing, on its way to San Francisco or Sydney or Singapore. Otherwise, it looked as if the Quest catamaran and its crew were the only inhabitants of the world.

"Guess I slept late," Jonny said to Jessie.

"Guess you did," she said. "Reading late as usual. Come and see! We're getting the submersible ready."

Following Jessie, Jonny raced to the stern (even though running on deck was STRICTLY FORBIDDEN) where he saw Bannon, Hadji, and Dr.

Quest working around a transparent plastic globe, about six feet in diameter.

"What's that?" Jonny asked.

"This is our sub," Hadji called back over his shoulder. He was helping the two men load oxygen tanks, which were stashed behind the twin bucket seats inside.

"Submarine?" Jonny asked. "Looks more like a soap bubble to me."

"Submersible," said his dad. "We don't call it a submarine because it doesn't travel under its own power. We lower it from the catamaran on a cable. It's more like an old-fashioned diving bell than a submarine."

"Let's call it the Belle," said Jessie. "The Belle of the Deep!"

"Suits me," said Dr. Quest. "What do you think, Race?"

"I like it," said Bannon. "A good vessel needs a good name."

"As you can see," said Dr. Quest, "there are two seats inside, plus a powerful electric heater, a video camera, halogen spotlights, and fuel cells, which are longer-lasting and more powerful than batteries. The Belle can descend safely to 3,000 feet. With Hadji and myself inside, it will drop down the cliff beside the Chatham Rise, spotlighting and videotaping the rocks. Hopefully, we will spot the giant squid in his lair."

"*Her* lair," corrected Jessie. "I thought you said the female was the real giant."

"Her lair, then," said Dr. Quest. "I stand corrected. *She* rarely comes to the surface, so if we wish to study her, we will have to do her the courtesy of calling on her at home."

Hadji came up out of the cabin wearing an insulated orange-and-black jumpsuit.

"You look like Halloween candy," said Jessie.

"Trick or treat," Hadji said, grinning.

"Why the insulated jumpsuits?" asked Jonny Quest. "This is the South Pacific, not the South Pole."

"The water is icy cold in the depths, even here," said Dr. Quest, pulling on his own black-and-orange jumpsuit. "With the suits, we can keep the heat low and reduce the drain on the fuel cells. We'll need all the power we can spare for the lights and the video camera. And now . . . "

He opened the oval door at the "front" of the sphere and stepped in. Hadji climbed in behind him.

Jonny Quest felt a moment of envy, disappointed that he wasn't going. But he knew it would pass.

Dr. Quest and Hadji sat in the twin seats. Hadji gripped the controls for the video camera while Dr. Quest handled the controls for the lights.

He tested the spotlight, shining it on the water. It seemed weak, compared to the bright sun.

"All systems ready," Dr. Quest said, his voice

crackling through the speaker on the communications control board.

Race Bannon started the winch.

"Good luck!" Jessie and Jonny said together.

Bannon slapped his great hand on the clear Plexiglas *Belle*. The winch whined and a crane lifted the *Belle* off the deck and swung it out over the water.

Jonny saw his father and Hadji waving as the submersible hit the water with a gentle splash—and disappeared under the water.

It's like living in two worlds at once, Jonny thought.

All around him was the bright blue sky and sea, warm with sunshine. On the control board monitor, however, he saw a world of darkness, lit by the occasional flicker of a passing fish.

It looked like a public-television nature show. Only what was on the monitor wasn't a TV show. It was real—it was the live video signal sent back by Hadji.

Jonny and Jessie stood at the control board, with Bandit between them, watching the screen on the monitor get darker and darker as the *Belle* dropped farther and farther into the depths, away from the familiar light of day.

"It's getting dark down here," said Hadji, his voice crackling over the speaker. "Dark as the caves of Malabar."

"Where's the mike?" Jonny asked.

"We're all on a speakerphone," said Race Bannon from the stern, where he was operating the winch. "Just talk up. They can hear you."

"Hadji, Dad—can you hear me?" Jonny asked.

"Of course," said Dr. Quest.

"You're breaking our eardrums!" said Hadji.

"Why don't you turn on the spotlight?" Jessie asked.

"I want to save the fuel cells," said Dr. Quest. "There won't be much to see until we get to the top of the Chatham Rise, almost a thousand feet down."

The winch whined, lowering the cable straight into the water.

Jonny watched it unwind. It was only about a half inch thick. It was hard to believe that there were two people at the end of it.

Two very important people!

"Look, it's snowing!" Hadji said as a glittering cloud of tiny white fish swam into view, and then out again.

"We have a visitor!" said Dr. Quest, his voice booming over the speakers.

On the monitor, a huge dim shape emerged from the darkness. Jonny recognized the ray, or another one just like it.

Then it was gone.

"What was that?" asked Jessie.

"It's our friend, the giant ray," said Jonny.

"Our friend, we hope!" said Hadji.

"Woof woof!" said Bandit.

"It's so weird talking like this," said Jessie. "It's like we are all in the same room—but we're up here, and you are way down there."

"No weirder than a telephone conference call," said Jonny. "You just have to get used to it."

The depth counter at the top right-hand corner of the screen went higher and higher as the submersible went deeper and deeper:

378

397

410

"Are those feet or meters?" Jessie asked.

"Or fathoms?" echoed Jonny.

"Feet," said Race Bannon. "At sea, depths can be measured in feet, meters, and fathoms. Watch this."

He left the winch and stepped up to the control board. He toggled a switch on the keyboard, and the display changed to fathoms (72) and then meters (241), then back to feet: 433.

"Neat!" Jessie said.

"How deep are they planning to go?" Johnny asked.

"All the way to 3,000 feet if necessary," Race Bannon said. "Whatever it takes to find the lair of the giant squid."

"Something's coming up!" said Hadji on the speaker. "It looks like—"

"I'm turning on the spotlight!" said Dr. Quest.

Jonny was trembling with excitement. He squeezed Jessie's arm as the spotlight revealed a mass of wriggling arms and tentacles—which soon resolved itself into a massive drifting clump of seaweed.

"False alarm," said Hadji. Did he sound disappointed, or was that Jonny's imagination?

"A kelp forest," said Dr. Quest, as the spotlight played across the gray-green fronds. "We would find lots of interesting sea life in there. But not what we are looking for."

The depth indicator continued to climb.

The *Belle of the Deep* continued to sink.

At 662 feet there were more clumps of seaweed, with fish swimming in and out of them, like cows grazing along the edge of a forest.

Then the monitor revealed what looked like a hilltop, covered with trees.

Dr. Quest shined his spotlight on it as the *Belle* dropped swiftly by.

The rocky ledge was covered with barnacles and shells, sponges and odd spiny plants.

"Slow us down, Race," said Dr. Quest. "That peak means we must be approaching the plateau."

The *Belle* dropped past another peak, this one covered with starfish and mollusks.

"The plants and animals here feed on the bits of

decaying dead fish that drop down from above," said Dr. Quest.

"Thanks for sharing," said Hadji.

"Ugh!" said Jessie.

"They'd probably say the same if they saw our diet," said Race.

"Particularly yours," Jessie whispered to Jonny, knowing his attraction to junk food.

"That's what we call the food chain," said Dr. Quest, slipping into his lecture mode. "Crabs and lobsters feed on the starfish and mollusks. Fish eat the crabs. Bigger fish eat the fish, and bigger fish eat them. All the way up to the giant squid."

"Or down," said Hadji.

"What eats the giant squid?" Jonny asked.

"Maybe the sperm whale," said Dr. Quest, his voice crackling over the speakerphone. "But we don't know for sure."

Soon the depth counter read 850. There were a few more peaks, and then the spotlight showed a mud plain, carved here and there with gullies and crevices.

"Slow us down, Race. We've reached the plateau."

Jonny and Jessie watched on the monitor as Dr. Quest played the spotlight along the broken plain, searching for the edge of the cliff.

"Got it!" he said finally. "We're in the perfect position, Race. Lower us on down."

The monitor showed the cliffside rushing past as the *Belle* was lowered. Occasionally it brushed the fronds of a kelp plant, sending up clouds of silt.

Jonny and Jessie (and Bandit) watched the monitor breathlessly as Dr. Quest's powerful spotlight illuminated undersea crags and cliffs, with colorful fish darting in and out.

"I'm glad we're getting all this on videotape," said Race Bannon.

"Tape? Never thought of it!" said Hadji.

"What!?"

"Don't let him kid you, Dad," said Jessie. She rapped the control board with her knuckles. "It's being stored right here, on CD."

Jonny tried to hide his smile, but he couldn't help laughing.

Tape! Sometimes Race Bannon was *so* old-fashioned!

The winch groaned as the cable dropped lower and lower into the sea. *Oddly,* thought Jonny, *it seems to be always the same length—twenty feet, from the end of the crane to the surface of the water.* Only by watching closely could he see that it was unwinding, dropping steadily.

At lunchtime, Jonny followed Jessie down to the galley to make sandwiches, while Race Bannon stayed and watched the winch and the depth gauge.

"Dad likes to worry," Jessie said, spreading peanut butter and jelly on bread slices.

21

"Somebody on the boat needs to worry," Jonny said. "That way the people in the *Belle* don't need to. At least that's the way I figure it."

"Are you worried?"

"Not really. Whatever happens down there, Dad and Hadji will be able to handle it."

Even as he spoke, Jonny wondered if he really believed what he was saying.

"Incredible!" he heard as they came back up. It was Hadji's voice, crackling over the speaker.

Jonny and Jessie raced to the control board. On the monitor, they saw that the *Belle* had dropped into a more verdant zone. The rocks were thick with starfish and seaweed. Huge fish stared out of holes in the cliff. Elegant jellyfish floated by, glowing in the spotlight, their transparent tentacles waving in the current.

"It's like another world!" said Jonny.

"It *is* another world," said Dr. Quest, over the speaker. "It's three-fourths of our world, and almost totally unknown to us. Most of the species on our planet live here, in the ocean depths. We know less about our own planet than we do about the moon."

The display at the top of the monitor read "1112."

The face of the undersea cliff was rocky, and covered with ferns and strange fish.

Then . . .

"What's that?!" Dr. Quest's deep voice rumbled over the control board speaker.

The spotlight jerked around, playing across the rocks, and Jonny saw a warship balanced on a cliff ledge.

It was covered with barnacles and weeds, but he could make out the name:

USS *Constance*

"I think I have heard of the *Constance*," said Race Bannon, who was watching from his station at the winch. "A World War II troopship that was lost to a Japanese submarine."

"I hope the men got out okay," Hadji said.

"The fighting was mostly to the north," said Dr. Quest. "But there were some engagements down here. Japanese subs preying on allied convoys."

"Look!" said Jessie.

The spotlight was illuminating a wooden clipper ship wedged into a ravine in the cliff side. Its three masts were broken into stumps.

"All the eras of sea travel are mixed down here," said Dr. Quest. "It's as if time were stopped; here we have two ships from two different centuries, almost side by side."

And there was more to come.

After a long blank section, the spotlight illuminated a twin-engine bomber, settled onto a shoulder of silt as if it had landed there.

Only the bullet holes around the shattered cockpit

and the skeleton sitting inside showed what had happened.

"A Betty," said Race Bannon, studying it on the monitor as the *Belle* dropped by.

"One of ours?" Jonny asked.

"If by *ours*, you mean *human*, yes," Dr. Quest said over the speaker. "If you mean *American*, no. The Betty was a Japanese dive-bomber. But from down here, in the depths, our petty wars seem far away, don't they?"

Race Bannon grunted without answering. Jonny could tell that he didn't agree. Even though he hadn't fought in World War II, Race Bannon's Navy loyalties were strong.

"Thirteen hundred, forty-three feet," called out Jessie, who was reading the depth gauge at the top of the monitor.

"You have 1600 more feet," Bannon said.

"To the end of the cable?" asked Jonny.

"The end of the cable and the end of the *Belle*'s safe submersible range," said Dr. Quest over the speakerphone. "At greater depths, the pressure would crush us. Slow us down, Race. I think I see something up ahead."

"Looks like snakes!" said Hadji. "Like the dance of Shiva, the ZXXSZXXZ of destruction and regeneration. . . ."

"Static!" said Jessie. She started throwing switches, trying to clear up the radio signal.

There was static on the monitor, too. The video was snowy. Then it cleared up and Jonny could see an approaching shadow, waving tentacles . . .

"Hey!"

Race and Hadji both spoke at once—one from the deep and one standing on deck.

On the monitor, Jonny could see giant gray-green tentacles pressing against the Plexiglas.

"We have found our prey," said Dr. Quest, his voice unnaturally calm.

"Or he's found you," said Race Bannon.

"How are you so sure it's a *he*?" asked Jessie.

Jonny admired her cool. His own heart was pounding!

3

"IT'S AT LEAST FIFTY FEET LONG!" SAID DR. QUEST.

"A hundred feet!" breathed Jonny.

The tentacles groping at the *Belle* were a foot in diameter, each studded with mouth-like suckers that stuck to the Plexiglas, then backed off—

"It's moving away!" said Hadji.

"Lower us faster, Race, so we can follow," said Dr. Benton Quest. "Keep the camcorder on it, Hadji!"

"What's *she* doing?" Jessie asked.

"Going down the cliff side," said Jonny. "They're trying to follow."

The winch whined and dropped the *Belle* faster. Dr. Quest and Hadji followed the giant squid with the spotlight and the camcorder. Far above, on the surface, the other members of the Quest Team caught glimpses of a gray-green creature bigger than a stretch limo, gliding swiftly through the murky water, dragging its tentacles behind it.

"It's going backward!" said Jonny. Then he realized that the rocket-shaped portion he had thought was the tail was actually the front.

"Faster, Race!" said Dr. Quest. "We need to get in closer for better video."

"Are you sure that's a good idea?" asked Bannon. But he increased the winch speed so that the cable was sinking into the water—

1487

1556

1598

The depth counter flickered as the *Belle* dropped deeper and deeper.

"Keep videotaping," said Dr. Quest to Hadji.

"Aye, aye, sir," Hadji answered. Jonny could hear the excitement in his friend's voice, and he couldn't help feeling slightly jealous.

If only I could be there! he thought. *All this excitement, and I have to watch it on TV!*

The monitor showed a huge creature with ten tentacles, each as big around as an elephant's trunk and several times as long.

"It looks to be about fifty, maybe sixty feet in length," said Dr. Quest, his voice crackling over the speaker. "Lower us faster, Race. We need to stay close to our friend."

"Are you so sure he's friendly?" Race asked.

"Are you so sure it's a *he?*" Jessie put in.

"Good point, Jessie," said Dr. Quest. "Judging

from the size, I would say this giant squid has to be a female. It's the biggest one that has ever been seen, or at least recorded. In fact, I—"

"Excuse me," said Jonny. Looking away from the monitor to rest his eyes, he had seen something that had disturbed him.

"Ssshhhhhhh!" said Race Bannon. "Don't interrupt Dr. Quest while he's talking."

"But look!" said Jonny.

He pointed toward the southern horizon. Jessie and Race Bannon both turned away from the monitor to look. A line of dark clouds stood like a wall marking the far edge of the world.

To Jonny they looked like storm clouds.

Big storm clouds.

"That storm is miles away," said Race Bannon. "Don't worry about it. We need to concentrate on what's happening here."

As if to call them back, Dr. Quest's voice came crackling over the speaker.

"I see light ahead!"

"Light?" Jonny and Jessie looked at each other, amazed. "How is that possible?"

"And it's getting warmer," said Hadji.

"The light seems to be coming from luminescent kelp growing around cracks in the cliff side," said Dr. Quest.

"Lumi-what?" Race Bannon whispered. The big man had a problem with big words.

"Luminescent. It means glow-in-the-dark," said Jessie.

The *Belle* was at 1625 feet, over half its rated depth of 3000, when Dr. Quest called out, "Slow us down. It seems to be stopping."

"I see a cave," Hadji put in excitedly.

Dr. Quest played the spotlight across the cliff face, and Hadji followed with the camcorder.

The giant squid was drifting slowly, paused in front of a dark hole in the cliff.

The whole scene was lit dimly by the luminescent fronds of the kelp, and occasionally by the flash of a glowing fish as it swam by.

"The water is definitely warmer here," said Dr. Quest. "I'm getting a reading of almost forty degrees."

"It should be much colder at that depth," said Race. "Wonder what's up?"

"This seems to be a vent area," said Dr. Quest. "Undersea volcanic vents. Sources of heat, and perhaps sources of water and gases as well. Perhaps that also accounts for the luminescent plant life."

"How's that?" asked Jonny.

"The vents attract many strange forms of plant and animal life," said Dr. Quest. "Some scientists even think they may be the original source of life. The vents may furnish the key to the squid's place in the food chain. The giant squid feeds on the life that breeds around the vents."

"Whatever," said Hadji. "Let's get closer, so I can get more video."

The creature was backing into the entrance of the cave. Only its tentacles could be seen, waving in the current, as if beckoning the submersible to come closer.

"She's inviting them in for tea," Jessie said.

Jonny looked at her in surprise. He could tell she was only half kidding.

"The water coming out of the cave is warm," Dr. Quest said, as the *Belle* dropped closer to the entrance. "Judging from the XZXZXZXZX, I would XXZXZXZXZXZX the vents. In fact, XXZXZXZXZXZXZXXXZZZZXXZ"

"Can't hear you!" shouted Race Bannon. "Too much static."

"Closer," said Dr. Quest. "Take us XZXZ-XZXZXZXZXZXZX."

"We're losing our signal!" said Jessie, spinning the dials on the control board. "The radio gets cut off if they get under the cliff."

"XXXZXZXZXZXZ magnificent!" said Dr. Quest. "But what's that?"

"XZXZXZ what?" Hadji asked, his voice almost lost in the static.

"Over XXZXZXZXZX!" The spotlight flashed through the water, and into the cave.

Something was coming out, racing toward them in a cloud of silt and sand.

Something huge.

"Look out!" yelled Jessie.

"Holy hopping admirals!" cried Race Bannon, who was standing behind Jonny and Jessie, looking over their shoulders at the monitor.

Emerging from the racing cloud was a tentacle as big around as a tree trunk.

It was followed by another, and another.

And then by a wriggling mass, in the center of which was a sharp beak, opening and closing.

"A *gianter* giant squid!" Jonny said.

"It's the *mama* squid!" breathed Jessie.

"It's XZXZXZXXZXZXZXZX fast," said Dr. Quest on the speakerphone. "Pull us up! Quick!"

Race Bannon ran to the stern of the boat. Jonny could hear gears clashing as Race struggled to stop and then reverse the winch.

On the speakerphone, there was a squeal: "Hurry and ZXZXZXZX!" said Dr. Quest. "I see a XZXZXZXZXZXZXZX . . . "

"We're losing our signal!" said Jessie.

Suddenly huge tentacles filled the monitor, slapping up against the Plexiglas of the submersible. Each tentacle was as thick as a man's body. Each pulsating hideous sucker was as big as a saucer.

Even though they were a quarter of a mile above

the action, in the sunlight and air, Jonny and Jessie jumped backward in fright instinctively.

"It's pulling them into the cave!" shouted Jonny.

"ZXZXZXZXZXZXZXZXZX!" came Dr. Quest's voice over the speaker.

The spotlight was brighter than ever on a mass of coiling tentacles.

Then the tentacles were gone, and the video showed a black disk the size of a basketball.

A disk as black and as cold as death itself.

Jonny shuddered. "What's *that?*" he gasped. "Could it be . . . ?"

"It is!" said Jessie. "It's an eye."

4

"THEY'RE IN TROUBLE!" RACE BANNON SAID. "GET US SOME sound, Jessie. Fast!"

Jessie's hands danced across the control board as she turned dials and switches, trying to modulate the sound signal from the *Belle*.

Jessie was an electronics wizard, usually able to fix or operate any radio, computer, or video. But now she was getting nothing but static.

"Dr. Quest, Hadji, can you hear me?" she shouted into the speakerphone.

Meanwhile Jonny stared, fascinated, at the huge black eye. It seemed to be looking out of the monitor, at him. Not only at him, but through him, into his very soul.

"We've lost the signal!" cried Jessie.

As she spoke, the giant black eye was enveloped in a cloud of snow, and then static.

"Hadji? Dad?" Jonny breathed.

The screen went dark.

There was one final burst of static from the

speaker, an ear-splitting squeal that was almost like a scream.

And then silence.

Jonny and Jessie looked at each other. Jonny could see the alarm on his face reflected in Jessie's.

"Reversing cable!" cried Race Bannon, behind them. "I'm bringing them up!"

The winch groaned. The deck tilted underneath Jonny's feet. He fell into Jessie, and they both rolled toward the side of the catamaran.

The boat was tilting! The cable was pulling it down!

Only the rope railing stopped Jonny and Jessie from plunging over the side, into the sea.

"Hang on!" shouted Race Bannon.

"Woof!" barked Bandit, sliding across the deck, toward the water.

Jessie grabbed the little dog at the last instant and held him under her arm.

Jonny could hear cogs clash as Race slipped a gear on the winch to let the cable freewheel.

The boat slowly righted itself. Jessie and Jonny ran to the stern and stood beside Race, watching the cable race into the water.

"It's still pulling them under!" shouted Jonny Quest. "You've got to stop it."

Race hit the cable brake, and the boat tipped dangerously.

He released the brake and let the cable run free again.

"We can't hold them!" he said. "Something has got them. Something big. And it's taking them to the bottom!"

The three members of the Quest Team—Jonny, Jessie, and Race Bannon—looked at one another in quiet alarm.

"Can we tell how deep they are?" Jonny asked.

"Not without our radio and video signal," Jessie said. She banged on the control board in frustration. "I can't even pick them up on my locater."

The monitor was all snow. The speaker was all static.

"What can we do?" Jonny and Jessie asked, almost in unison.

Race Bannon shrugged his massive shoulders. "Wait."

The only sound was the lapping of the waves and the low whine of the unreeling cable.

The bright blue of the sky and sea was a stark contrast to the cold and darkness Jonny knew was endangering his father and his friend and adopted brother, far below.

The scene on the boat was calm—a calm that would have seemed strange to anyone not familiar with the Quest Team.

When disaster struck, instead of panicking, they grew calmer. It was a discipline that had paid off in hundreds of tight spots. Jonny only hoped that it would pay off again. He had confidence in himself and in Race and Jessie—as well as in his dad and Hadji, far below.

The cable disappeared into the water like time itself—unchanging and yet ever changing; going and yet never going. *Hadji would like this,* Jonny thought, visualizing his friend, whose spiritual nature loved paradoxes and parables.

"How deep can they go?" Jessie asked.

"To the end of the cable" her dad answered. "Three thousand feet. Then it will either stop, or pull the boat under—"

Or break, Jonny thought. But he kept the thought to himself.

Suddenly the deck shuddered and they all three stumbled.

"Woof, woof!" barked Bandit.

The cable spool on the winch was empty.

The stern of the boat dipped, farther and farther, until the water washed up over the deck.

Then it rose slightly—and stopped.

"End of the cable," said Race Bannon.

They all held their breaths, waiting for the cable to pull the catamaran under.

"Three thousand feet," said Race. "They can't go much deeper without—"

He didn't say the rest. *Being crushed by the pressure*, Jonny thought.

"Maybe it let them go," Jessie suggested.

Race Bannon reversed the gears and tried winching the cable back in. The winch groaned and the cable grew taut, and the boat dipped—but the cable wouldn't budge.

"Stuck," Race said.

"How much air do they have?" Jonny asked.

"Another two and a half hours."

"One of us has to go down," said Jonny and Jessie almost in unison.

Ten minutes later Jonny Quest, dressed in thermal long johns, was zipping himself into a pressurized diving suit.

"Dad needs to be up here operating the winch," said Jessie. "I'm the best with the radio and video."

"Woof, woof."

"And we need Bandit for moral support. That means you are the only one we can spare!"

Jonny smiled at her joke. They both knew he was eager to get into the action, wherever it might take him.

Race Bannon handed Jonny a sleek helmet. Jonny put it on but left the faceplate open.

"This is a special free-dive deepsuit," said Bannon. "I helped your father design it. It is good for three thousand feet. We'll just hope they aren't stuck any further down than that."

37

"Woof, woof," said Bandit.

"I agree," said Jessie.

"Just watch out for the storm," Jonny said. He pointed toward the horizon. The wall of clouds looked darker, higher—and closer than before.

"Leave the worrying to us," said Race, as he attached fresh batteries and oxygen tanks to the back of the suit.

"Those tanks look small," said Jessie.

"They will last three hours," said Race. "The suit is equipped with a rebreather."

"What's a rebreather?" asked Jessie, who wasn't afraid to ask questions. "Only a fool pretends to know everything," Dr. Quest always said.

"It's a scrubber system that takes the CO_2 out of the air," said Jonny. "It makes the oxygen last longer. And it cuts down on the bubbles so you don't make a lot of commotion and scare the fish."

He closed the faceplate. "Can you hear me?" he asked.

"Plain as day," said Jessie, speaking into the speakerphone. "I'm going to lock onto you with a beeper, too, so we will know your position."

"Good," said Jonny, relieved. He tried to take a step. It was almost impossible to move in the deepsuit.

"This thing sure is stiff," he said.

"It'll be better in the water," said Race Bannon. "It's not made for walking around."

38

He and Jessie helped Jonny to the side of the catamaran.

"Follow the cable down," said Race. "That way you can't get lost. And watch your depth! There is a depth gauge on your wrist—that LCD readout."

"Cool," said Jonny. He looked down at the water. He could feel his courage start to fade. He knew better than to wait around.

"I'm ready," he said.

"PROCEED WITH CAUTION," Jessie said. Jonny grinned. It was their private joke. When they were nervous, they cut the tension by talking in "road sign."

"RESUME SAFE SPEED," said Jonny.

Race patted Jonny on the shoulder. It was strange watching his lips move and hearing his voice over the radio.

"Good luck," Race said.

Jonny leaned over the side, looking for the ladder they used for swimming and working on the hull. But it was on the other side of the boat.

"Should we get the ladder?" Jonny asked.

Race Bannon shook his head. He pointed toward the deep blue of the Pacific.

"Jump," he said.

Jonny jumped.

5

MINUTES LATER JONNY QUEST WAS DROPPING INTO THE depths alongside the cable.

"Can you hear me?" Jessie asked, over the deepsuit's radio.

"Loud and clear," said Jonny.

"How do you feel?" Race asked.

"Fine," said Jonny. "The suit seems to be working perfectly."

"There's a ballast adjustment on your wrist," said Race. "Turn it to the left to drop faster, to the right to drop slower. How deep are you now?"

Jonny checked the LCD readout on his wrist controller.

"Two hundred and twenty-five feet," he said.

"That's about right," said Race. "If you hold that rate you'll be okay."

"MAINTAIN SAFE SPEED," said Jessie.

For Jonny, it was like being in two worlds at once. The voices on the deepsuit's radio linked him to a familiar warm, blue world of light and air.

40

But all around him was an unfamiliar world of cold and darkness.

Getting colder.

Getting darker.

Reaching for his wrist controller, Jonny turned on the suit's battery-powered heater, which automatically compensated for the water temperature.

Another switch turned on the helmet light. By turning his head, and directing the helmet's spotlight, Jonny was able to see in any direction he could look.

The problem was, there was nothing to see.

Nothing but the cable, disappearing above into the fading blue of the surface, and below into the growing darkness.

"See anything?" Jessie asked.

Jonny was just about to say no when he passed through a school of tiny fish, flashing silver in the beam of his helmet light.

Then in the distance he saw the dark mass of a sperm whale, as large as a cloud itself.

"Lots," he said. "There's lots to see."

As he dropped into the depths, Jonny marveled at the diversity of life. Some creatures of the sea were tiny, some were huge; some were a hundred thousand times as large as others; yet all contained the same spark and desire to live that he had.

Truly, all life on earth is one, he thought.

As he dropped past 391 feet, Jonny saw his old friend, the giant ray, in the distance, a shadow in the eternal twilight of the deep.

Closer, he saw a sea turtle, the size of a dining room table, paddling lazily to who knew where, comfortable in the knowledge that it was protected by its shell.

"Jonny, you okay?" Race's voice boomed in the deepsuit's speaker.

"Sure. Why?"

"Just checking. We don't want you drifting off into the ecstasy of the deep," Race said.

"What's that?" Jessie asked, her voice crackling through the speaker alongside her father's.

"Sometimes divers get so caught up in the beauty of the sea that they never want to come up," Race said. "It can be like a mystical experience."

"Don't worry about me," said Jonny. "I'll leave all that mystical stuff for Hadji."

But he realized he *had* been caught up in the ecstasy. He hadn't been paying close attention to what was happening around him. He had forgotten the first rule of the Quest Team—stay alert.

The farther Jonny dropped into the sea, the darker it got. He passed through hanging forests of seaweed, and looking up he saw the surface of the ocean, shining silver, gleaming like a bank of clouds.

And as far away.

"How deep are you?" Jessie asked, her voice sounding warm, right in his ear.

Jonny checked the LCD readout on his wrist controller.

"Eight hundred and sixty-five feet."

"You should be seeing the first signs of the Chatham Rise," Race said.

Jonny turned around and saw the rocky peak his father and Hadji had seen.

"Right you are," he said.

Still following the cable, Jonny descended to the top of the plateau. It was a mud plain broken with ravines. In one of the ravines he saw the remains of a three-masted cargo ship, from the last days of the great sailing vessels, when they were made of iron instead of wood.

The masts had almost rusted away. Streams of rust hung down the side of the ship like orange beards.

"What temperature are you showing?" Race asked.

Jonny checked the temperature readout on his wrist controller.

"Thirty-seven degrees," he said, repressing a shiver, even though it was warm in his suit.

"Any sign of the vents Dr. Quest and Hadji saw?"

"Not yet," said Jonny. "But they were down the side of the cliff. I'm just reaching the edge right now."

"You sound like you are right here with us," Jessie said.

"Good," Jonny said. "It means the radio is working right. What about that storm we saw?"

"No problem," she said. "It's just hanging there on the horizon."

Actually, Jessie was worried.

The clouds on the horizon were getting bigger and darker— and closer.

The waves, which had been a light chop, were getting bigger, too. The cable was creaking as the catamaran rose and fell on the swells.

Race worked with the winch, trying to get more slack. But the cable was played all the way out; there was no way to reduce the tension.

It would be a double disaster if the cable broke, Jessie thought. She looked from her father's worried face to the dark clouds, slowly moving closer and closer.

"Everything's fine up here," she repeated. "Just PROCEED WITH CAUTION down there."

"Woof, woof," added Bandit.

Jonny slowed his descent by adjusting the ballast on his suit with the wrist controller.

He checked his depth: 892 feet.

He paused on the edge of the cliff and, with his helmet light, followed the arc of the cable as it disappeared over the side of the rocky undersea plateau.

"I'm on the edge of the plateau," he said, just to hear his own voice.

"How deep are you?" Jessie asked.

Jonny was glad to hear her voice. It was like a ray of sunshine in the darkness that surrounded him.

"Nine hundred and twelve feet," he said.

"Are you still following the cable?" Race asked.

"Affirmative," said Jonny. With his helmet light, Jonny peered over the edge, following the cable as far as he could before it disappeared into the darkness.

Do I really want to go down there? he thought.

Then he thought of his father and Hadji in danger.

"I'm going over the edge," he said. "I will continue going down."

Adjusting the ballast to make himself "heavier," Jonny stepped off into the darkness.

At 1155 feet Jonny passed the sunken American troopship. A little deeper, the clipper ship his father and Hadji had seen.

"Still on course," he said.

He passed the Japanese dive-bomber and resisted the impulse to wave at the skeleton seated in the shattered cockpit.

Far below he saw a faint glow of light.

"I can see light ahead, just like Dad and Hadji saw," Jonny said. "And it does seem to be getting warmer."

"How much warmer?" asked Race Bannon.

"I'm at 39 degrees."

"PASS WITH CARE," Jessie said.

"Will do."

The ledges along the cliff were covered with mud and silt that had filtered down over the centuries. *How many sailors' and fishermen's bones are buried under all that mud?* Jonny wondered. As he dropped past he thought of all the New England whalers, and the Maoris in their outrigger canoes, all trying to get a living from the unforgiving sea.

As he dropped, Jonny was alert for predators. But except for a few lurking shadows far off—which might be hammerhead sharks—the cliff side was clear.

It was crowded with life, though. Ferns and seaweed of many colors clung to the rocks, and back in the clefts Jonny could see eyes and tentacles and feelers. Creepy crawly things were waiting. Jonny imagined claws and snappers, tentacles and antennae, and he shivered.

The seaweed, waving in the current, was red. Jonny turned off his helmet light.

He could still see it.

"The plants here are luminescent," Jonny said. "They glow in the dark."

"You must be approaching the vent area," Race said, from far above. "Does it feel any warmer?"

46

"Maybe a little," Jonny said. He checked his readout. "Yes, it's almost up to 44 degrees. And I'm at 1523 feet."

"I think you have found the undersea vent area," said Race. "It's like a warm spring under the sea. Water warmed by volcanic activity, hot springs."

"Like Old Faithful at Yellowstone," put in Jessie.

"Exactly," said Race. "And they attract all sorts of sea life, like Dr. Quest said."

"WILDLIFE CROSSING," said Jessie.

"I Brake for Animals," said Jonny.

"What are you two talking about?" Race asked, exasperated.

"Nothing," Jonny and Jessie said together, both giggling.

"The cave," Jonny said, as much to himself as to his comrades on the surface. He slowed his descent by adjusting his ballast.

"Can you see any sign of Dr. Quest and Hadji?" Race asked.

"No, but I can see why we lost radio contact. The cable goes into the cave."

"I thought so," said Jessie.

"How big is the cave?" Race asked.

"Big enough," said Jonny. "You could drive a bus into it."

Or a giant squid, he thought.

47

"Can you see anything?" Jessie asked.

"Not really. It's dark back in there. I'm going to have to go in."

"ROUGH ROAD AHEAD," Jessie said.

"Don't worry, I'll YIELD RIGHT OF WAY," Jonny said. He swam into the cave entrance.

The cave was about fifty feet wide and a hundred feet high. Jonny shined his helmet light toward the back.

The cable disappeared around a bend, into the darkness.

"It looks pretty deep," Jonny said.

There was no answer.

"Jessie? Race? You there?"

Still no answer.

Jonny swam back out to the entrance. As soon as he emerged from the cave, he heard Jessie's worried voice: "Where have you been? I lost you on the locater."

"I was in the cave. I guess it blocks the signal."

"See anything?" Race Bannon asked.

"Not yet," Jonny said. "I'll have to go deeper. It means we'll be out of radio contact."

"I don't know," said Race. "It may not be XXZXZXZXZXZ"

Jonny didn't hear the rest. With a flick of his wrist controller, he started the suit's tiny twin propellers and pushed off into the darkness.

6

THE CAVE NARROWED AS JONNY FOLLOWED THE CABLE around the first bend.

Then the cave turned upward. Jonny stopped to trim the ballast in his deepsuit before proceeding upward into the darkness.

He dimmed his helmet light to save his batteries, and glided slowly, cautiously, near the roof of the cavern. It was like a dream of flying.

Except it was really happening!

The rock walls glowed dimly. When Jonny turned down his helmet light even further, he could see phosphorescent moss in the cracks and tendrils of luminescent seaweed.

Now that he could no longer hear the encouraging voices of Race and Jessie, he felt the loneliness of the deep.

"Hello," he said, to himself.

"Hello," he said back.

Everything around him was strange, alien.

49

The rock walls with their waving tendrils of softly glowing seaweed had never seen sunlight. The scurrying crab-like creatures in the cracks, the sponges and starfish attached to the rock ledges had lived their quiet lives in dim obscurity.

Even more than before, Jonny marveled at the amazing diversity of life on planet earth.

"I am the alien here," he whispered to himself, wondering at the millions of ways living things cooperated and fought, seeking their food.

"It's wonderful, all right," he said to himself. "But not so wonderful that I want to become part of the food chain down here!"

He steadied his breathing, remembered his Quest Team alertness training, and took Jessie's "road sign" advice—PROCEED WITH CAUTION.

At every turn, Jonny expected to see the *Belle*, the tiny submersible with Hadji and his father inside.

And at every turn he was disappointed.

Jonny didn't lose hope, though. He knew how resourceful they both were. "I'm sure they are all right," he said to himself. It was good to hear a voice, even if it was his own!

After the first few turns, the glowing seaweed thinned out and the cave got dimmer and dimmer.

Darker and darker.

The cave was still going upward, though. Jonny

paused and read the depth meter on his wrist monitor: 1123.

Jonny had ascended several hundred feet since he had entered the cave. He knew he must be approaching the top of the plateau. *Was the cave merely a passageway to the top?* he wondered.

The temperature was holding steady at 44 degrees.

Then, as he followed the cable around another turn, Jonny noticed something *different* in the water around him.

It was just a slight stirring, a change in the way the particles danced in his helmet light. A subtle alteration in the way the seaweed waved in the current.

It was like the feeling in the summer before a thunderstorm, when the air is charged with energy.

It was no more than a feeling—but as a Quest Team member on adventures around the world, Jonny had learned to trust his instincts.

They weren't just *his* alone—they had been handed down to him by millions of years of evolution. They were his animal heritage, his survival tools.

Trust them, something told him. And trust them, Jonny did.

It was instinct that pulled him out of the main passageway, into a cleft in the side of the tunnel wall.

It was instinct that caused him to click off his helmet light.

Jonny could *feel* something approaching.

Then, in the dim light from the luminescent moss and seaweed, Jonny could *see* it.

Almost.

Or at least the cloud of dust and silt it raised.

A giant shadow came around the bend in the tunnel and sped past. Whatever it was—and Jonny had a pretty good idea *what* it was—it was twice the size of a city bus.

He saw darkness and movement, speed and power, and he saw something more—a kind of cold intelligence. A survival instinct that was equal to his own.

Then it was gone.

"The mama squid," Jonny said aloud, to himself. "The big one."

He had never felt so alone as when he was witnessing that vast inhuman mass of cold flesh. He wished more than ever that he could hear Jessie's voice, or Race's. He wanted nothing more than to see the sunlight, and feel the air on his skin.

He had never felt so trapped.

The giant squid had been heading toward the entrance, and so, for Jonny, there was only one way to go.

Deeper.

Into the cave.

*   *   *

"How deep are you, Jonny?"

Jonny checked the readout on his wrist controller.

"Eight hundred and seventy-six feet," he said.

"Is it getting any warmer?" Jonny asked.

"About the same," Jonny answered. "Forty-four degrees."

Jonny was talking to himself. It was his only weapon against the silence.

Since he had encountered the giant squid, he had followed the cable more slowly, pausing at every turn in the tunnel. It had gotten darker and darker the farther he had gone.

But now the tunnel seemed to be getting brighter again.

"I wonder if it's going to come out at the top of the plateau," Jonny said.

"Beats me," he answered himself. Then added in road sign language, "PROCEED WITH CAUTION."

There was a sharp turn, where the cave went around a boulder. When he turned this corner, Jonny saw a sight in his helmet light that brought his heart to his throat and made his skin crawl.

He saw the end of the cable.

The cable was wedged under a rock, and torn off. The broken end was waving in the slow current like a dead hand.

And the submersible, the *Belle of the Deep*, was gone!

"Dad!" Jonny said aloud. "Hadji!"

Where could they be? Could they possibly have survived this disaster?

Then Jonny looked up. He was at the end of the cave.

Above him the water seemed almost as bright as day.

Jonny twisted off the ballast on his wrist controller and shot upward, toward the light.

He broke through the surface of the water—but he was not at the surface of the sea.

In his helmet light, he could see rock walls all around him, covered with the now-familiar fronds of luminescent seaweed.

He was in a huge cavern, under the sea. But this cavern was filled with air, not water.

Adjusting his ballast control to "float," Jonny lifted his face mask and cautiously took a breath.

The air stank. It smelled like dead fish, but it was breathable.

He turned on his helmet light and looked around.

No sign of giant squid: That was the first thing!

As his eyes grew accustomed to the dim light, Jonny saw a sight that gave him hope.

At the far side of the cavern, almost a hundred

yards away, the familiar Plexiglas bubble of the *Belle* floated on top of the water.

The door was open. It was empty.

The *Belle* was wedged up against the side of a larger monster—a creature that Jonny thought at first was a whale.

It was a vessel, several hundred feet long, streaked with rust and covered with barnacles and lichens.

Jonny shined his helmet light on the boat as he approached cautiously. He recognized the markings from high-school history, even though he couldn't understand what it was doing here in the Pacific, ten thousand miles from its home waters.

For it was a World War II German submarine—a Nazi U-boat!

7

THE CAVERN WAS HUGE.

Jonny Quest was in a vast undersea room, at least three hundred feet in diameter, and twice that high. It was lighted on all sides by the luminescent ferns, which gave off a ghostly glow. Strange rock formations along the walls, like the statuary in a Gothic cathedral, gave the room an awesome grandeur.

But Jonny didn't have time to admire the weird beauty of the cave. He had to find out what had happened to his father and Hadji.

Using the electrical power of his deepsuit, he propelled himself across the surface of the water toward the side of the cave where the *Belle* was bobbing up against the seaweed-covered side of the Nazi U-boat. The script on the conning tower said U–232.

Jonny could see that the *Belle* had been abandoned in a hurry. The door was ajar, and the interior lights were still on. He was hopeful— obviously his dad and Hadji had gotten out.

But where had they gone? Perhaps onto the derelict U-boat.

Then, as Jonny got closer to the submarine, he saw that it wasn't as derelict as he had thought.

In the side of the hull was a small porthole. Through the seaweed and scum that covered it, Jonny could see a yellow light.

Someone—or something—was inside!

Moving carefully, pulling himself up by the thick fronds of kelp, Jonny climbed onto the deck of the submarine.

Walking slowly so that his footsteps wouldn't ring on the rusted deck, Jonny crept around the side of the conning tower. He leaned down and with his glove began to wipe away the weeds and scum that had covered the porthole.

Inside the submarine he could see a small room lit by a fluorescent light. Maps covered the walls.

Jonny stared wide-eyed at a gray-bearded skinny old man talking frantically. He was wearing a Nazi uniform. His left leg was a wooden peg.

His ancient, sallow skin was wrinkled and his hair and bushy eyebrows were snow white. He seemed to be laughing, and every laugh showed stained yellow teeth.

His right eye was covered with a white patch decorated with a black streak of lightning.

The old man was waving a gun. Jonny recognized it from the firearms recognition class he and Hadji and Jessie had taken with Race Bannon.

It was a Luger, the favorite automatic pistol of the so-called "master race."

But who was the old Nazi yelling at?

Ducking down so that he wouldn't be seen, Jonny Quest crossed to the other side of the porthole. From there he could see the rest of the room.

Two men were tied to chairs, bound and gagged with silver tape.

Or rather, one man and a teenager.

Both wearing black-and-orange jumpsuits—

Dr. Quest and Hadji!

Jonny's first feeling was one of relief. At least they hadn't been eaten by the giant squid, or drowned. Now that he knew that they were safe—so far, anyway—he realized he had a new problem.

How was he going to rescue them?

And even if he did, how was he going to get them to the surface?

Jessie stood at the bow of the Quest catamaran, looking over the rail. She was squinting. It was almost as if she believed that if she looked hard enough, she could see all the way to the bottom.

What was happening with Jonny? What was

happening with Dr. Quest and Hadji? Jessie felt she would give anything just for a few words over the radio.

But the radio on the control board was silent. It had been for almost an hour now.

"Hey kid!"

She turned. It was her dad. His smile was almost as broad as his shoulders.

"No point in worrying," he said. "Help me get the catamaran shipshape and trim the sails. We may be getting company."

"Company?"

Jessie followed her father's hand, pointing toward the horizon.

She had forgotten the storm. The last time she had seen it, it had looked like a faraway range of low, dark mountains.

Now that range was beginning to tower darkly.

It was much closer.

Jessie shivered. She hoped the storm didn't hit before all the members of the Quest Team were safe.

"Woof!" Bandit felt it, too.

Already, there was an ominous chill in the air.

Jonny backed away from the porthole, moving awkwardly. The deepsuit wasn't designed for operation out of the water.

He thought about taking it off, but where would

he put it? If something happened to the deepsuit, he would be trapped. Besides, he was wearing nothing underneath but his thermal long johns, and the cavern was chilly and damp.

His first problem was how to get into the submarine.

He climbed the rungs built into the side of the conning tower, looking for an entrance.

There was a door at the top, but Jonny was afraid to open it. Suppose it led straight into the chart room where the old man was holding Dr. Quest and Hadji at gunpoint?

No, surprise was Jonny's only weapon. He had to find another entrance.

Then he realized that the deepsuit was the key.

He climbed back down the conning tower, crossed the deck, and lowered himself into the water.

He closed his face mask and slipped underwater.

The bottom of the submarine was covered with kelp and barnacles, just like the top.

Using the deepsuit's electric power, Jonny swam to the bow of the sub.

He was in luck. The torpedo tubes were open. The torpedoes had all been fired. Johnny knew—from his studies with Race Bannon of famous naval vessels—that the tubes would lead into the torpedo room.

It was a way in.

* * *

Jonny squeezed into one of the four tubes. He found a wheel on a small door at the end, the torpedo loading door. It was almost as small as the door on Bandit's doghouse, back at the Quest compound.

For a brief moment, Jonny found himself wondering how faithful Bandit was doing. He wondered if he would ever see his dog again.

But there was no time for regrets—or fears.

Jonny turned the wheel on the loading door, and the door gave way under the water pressure.

Jonny was swept through it, into a small, cramped torpedo room.

Water spilled onto the metal floor, and washed up against the door leading from the torpedo room into the main part of the submarine.

Quickly, Jonny reached behind him and closed the loading door, sealing out the water.

Then he opened the faceplate on his helmet.

The air was musty. It smelled of death and age and war and time; it smelled terrible but it was breathable.

Jonny took off his helmet and, using it as a flashlight, looked around the room.

That was when he saw the German sailor.

He was sitting on the floor, leaning against the wall.

Staring at Jonny.

Grinning.

His grin was the grin of death, and his stare was

the stare of doom—for he was nothing but a skeleton in a German Navy uniform.

His stare and his grin were holes in a skull.

The dead sailor was wearing a Nazi uniform, with the jacket hung loosely over his shoulders.

Jonny stepped out of the clumsy deepsuit, and propped it against a torpedo rack.

"Excuse me," Jonny said, lifting the jacket off the skeleton's shoulder.

He put it on. It was an officer's jacket, with gold braid on the sleeves. On the shoulder was a patch: twin interlocked circles, the universal symbol of nuclear power, around a letter and some numbers, "U–232."

"Wonder what this means?" Jonny mused. "They didn't have nuclear subs back in World War II—or did they?"

Jonny Quest turned the wheel on the main torpedo room door. It opened with a groan.

Jonny stepped through, into a long narrow corridor filled with pipes and valves.

The corridor was lit with dim, flickering fluorescent lights. A 1945 calendar hung on the wall.

Where's the electrical power coming from? Jonny wondered. *After fifty years?*

Jonny closed the door behind him and tiptoed

along the corridor, feeling his way. The light was very dim, but he could see another door at the far end.

Halfway down the corridor Jonny hit something with his foot. He looked down.

It was another skeleton, this one stretched out on the floor. It was wearing a seaman's uniform—no braid.

"Excuse me," Jonny whispered, stepping over.

Light came under the door at the end of the hallway. Jonny could hear voices.

He turned the wheel on the door as slowly as possible. Even so, it creaked and groaned and squealed.

The element of surprise was gone. Jonny knew that as soon as he opened the door he would feel a bullet plowing into him.

But what choice did he have?

He had to save his father and Hadji if he could.

Maybe he could jump the old man before he had time to fire.

Jonny pushed with both hands, but the door was stuck.

Then it gave all at once, and he fell through, stumbling to his knees. Jonny looked up, wincing, expecting at any moment to feel a Luger bullet slice into him.

Instead, the old German was smiling.

"Heil Hitler," he said. "Welcome!"

8

"HUH?" JONNY SAID.

"Excuse me if I speak in English," said the ancient German. With his eye patch, he seemed to be winking. "But I wouldn't want to be rude to our guests. Have you met them?"

He waved the Luger toward Dr. Quest and Hadji, who were bound to chairs against the wall beside the porthole. In their orange-and-black jumpsuits, they were the brightest things in the room. Both were gagged with silver tape.

"They are spies," said the old German. "American spies! I caught them sneaking into the U-232 just today."

Jonny Quest looked at his father and Hadji. They both were rolling their eyes, telling him to play along with the old man with the gun.

"The American spies have, of course, never seen a nuclear submarine before!" the old man said.

"A nuclear sub!" Jonny said, under his breath.

Was it possible? He looked toward his father and caught a slight nod.

He looked down at the patch on his own shoulder.

So that was the meaning of the nuclear symbol!

"Who knows how long they have been watching us?" the old man went on. "I took this strange electrical spyglass from them."

He held up Hadji's videocamera!

Jonny could tell by the gleam in his eye and the frantic quality of his voice that the old man was mad. "As your *Kapitän,* I have cabled to U-boat *Überkommand* for instructions as to how to deal with these spies. Meanwhile, *Torpedokommander,* shut the door behind you and come on in."

"Uh, sure," Jonny muttered. He stepped the rest of the way into the room, carefully closing the door behind him.

He was in the control room of the German sub. There was a periscope in the center of the room, and a wheel and various levers and valves at the front.

Hadji and his dad's chairs were on the other side of it.

Filthy water slopped on the floor. The air smelled of sweat and grease and death.

Lots of death.

"Spies must die!" said the German captain. "We will execute them as soon as I get a confirmation from

SS Headquarters. Meanwhile, it gives us a chance to practice our English, *Ja, Torpedokommander?*"

"*Ja,*" Jonny said. "Whatever."

He edged slowly across the room toward his father and Hadji. He didn't want to alarm the captain, especially since he was holding a gun.

And was out of his skull!

"You watch our prisoners for a moment," said the captain. "I must go to the radio room next door and check for messages."

Jonny nodded.

The captain limped out of the room. With his peg leg, he looked like Captain Ahab or Long John Silver.

As soon as the control room door closed behind the captain, Jonny rushed to his father's side and pulled off the tape.

Then he pulled the tape off Hadji's mouth.

"Am I glad to see you!" Hadji said. "I thought we were goners!"

"The old nut has gone to check the radio," Dr. Quest said. "He checks it every five minutes, even though the tubes are dead and there are, of course, no messages. He doesn't know his precious Third Reich has been dead for fifty years. He doesn't even realize he's trapped in a cave. He's totally insane, but we have to play along with him, at least for now."

"We do?" said Jonny. He paused, untaping his father's hands. "Why can't we just jump him and take him out?"

"He's the only one who knows how to operate this sub," said Dr. Quest. "We need him to get to the surface. Or at least to get the boat started. I have no idea how it works. Imagine—a German nuclear sub from World War II!"

"I didn't think the Nazis had nuclear power in World War II," said Jonny.

"Neither did I," said Dr. Quest. "Apparently this sub was a top-secret prototype. The nuclear reactor was used to charge the batteries, which is why the boat still has electricity after fifty years."

"Fifty years!" said Jonny. "It's hard to believe that old man has been here all that time. How did that geezer manage to capture you? And where are we anyway?"

"One question at a time," said Dr. Quest, rubbing his wrists. "We were pulled under by a giant squid. As you may know."

"It was twice the size of the first one!" Hadji put in. "I was praying to Shiva and Buddha and Allah all at once."

"I know, I saw it on the video," Jonny said. "But then we lost radio and video contact."

"The squid dragged us into the cave, to the end of the cable," said Dr. Quest. "Then the cable got wedged under a rock and broke, and we floated up in here. This cavern is apparently a bubble formed by the gasses from the undersea vents. The vents keep the water relatively warm and keep the air relatively breathable. That's how the captain has been able to survive here for fifty years."

"Fifty years!" Jonny said again.

"From listening to the old man rave, I have learned that his name is Captain Grimm. The sub is the U–232. It was a secret prototype sent to help the Japanese prey on U.S. shipping. I expect Grimm was pulled under by the same giant squid that got us."

"Or maybe its grandmother," Hadji put in.

"But why?" Jonny asked.

Dr. Quest shrugged. "Who knows? Perhaps it is keeping us for food. Perhaps we're just little bright treasures lining its nest, like the pieces of tinfoil that sometimes turn up in birds' nests."

"When the *Belle* bobbed up in here, we thought we were goners," said Hadji. "Then we saw the sub."

"Of course, we assumed it was deserted," said Dr. Quest. "When we came down the hatch, the old captain was waiting."

"He beaned us both," Hadji said, rubbing the back of his head.

"When we came to, here we were, tied up," said Dr. Quest. "Captain Grimm has been talking non-stop ever since, in German and English. He thinks the crew is still alive. He talks to the skeletons. That's why he wasn't surprised when he saw you."

"But how has he survived all these years?" asked Jonny.

"The sub's nuclear reactor distills drinking water from the sea," said Dr. Quest. "And the air in the cavern is maintained by the vents."

"That explains air and water," said Jonny. "But what about food?"

"He has been living off the supplies for the whole crew," Dr. Quest said. "He has a huge supply of stuff called Aryan Health Cakes."

"Which reminds me," said Hadji. "I'm starving. Did you bring any bagels down with you?"

"Sssshhhh!" said Dr. Quest. "Here comes the captain! Leave the tape loose on our mouths and hands, so it will look like we are still tied up."

The waves rose and fell in giant, smooth swells.

The Quest catamaran was rising and falling with it, rising and falling.

Watching over the rail, Jessie thought the sea looked like a great monster breathing.

In and out, in and out.

The monster was asleep now. But soon it would awaken.

Judging from the towering dark clouds, looming closer and closer, it would awaken very soon.

"Woof, woof," said Bandit.

"I wish they were here, too," said Jessie. "But at least they know we are here, waiting for them."

The cable at the stern was creaking and groaning.

"If the waves get much bigger, we're in trouble, though," said Jessie. "With the cable holding our stern down, the waves will swamp us."

"Woof, woof," said Bandit.

Jessie looked at the approaching dark clouds, streaked with sudden lightning. The wind was rising. There was a chill in the air.

Jessie looked back to the catamaran's central control board, where Race Bannon was pushing buttons, hydraulically trimming the sails to keep the vessel pointed into the wind. For the first time Jessie noticed an axe, leaning against the winch.

"What's the axe for?" she asked.

"If the waves get too high, we'll have to cut the cable," Race said matter-of-factly.

"And leave them on the bottom?"

"Only as a last resort," said Race. "But come, help me secure the sails. We have to tighten up if we expect to ride out this blow!"

"*Heil* Hitler," said the captain, coming back into the chart room of the U-boat and closing the door behind him.

"Salute him," Jonny's father whispered.

Much as Jonny hated to, he saluted the demented white-haired captain.

Grimm grinned. "You spies will be glad to know that there is no shipping in sight. A few more pathetic Americans will enjoy the gift of life for a few more hours. Including yourselves: I have had no word from *Überkommand* on what they want to do with you. But I warn you, one false move and—"

He held the Luger to Hadji's head. Hadji closed his eyes as if going into his yogin meditation.

"—You will both be summarily executed!" the demented captain said in his heavily accented English.

Then he said something to Jonny in German.

"What's he saying?" Jonny asked.

"He says, 'Prepare the crew for action,'" whispered Dr. Quest. "He says, 'Prepare to dive.'"

"What do I do?" Jonny asked. "What do I say?"

"Nothing. He doesn't expect you to answer. He's been muttering to himself for fifty years. Let's just let him do his thing. Maybe he can take this ship down and out of this cave!"

The captain grabbed the wheel in the front of the room. He pulled a lever down, and Jonny heard a gurgling from the front of the ship.

"What's that noise?" Hadji whispered.

"Must be the ballast tanks filling," said Dr. Quest.

The captain hit a switch on the ship's control board, and Jonny was surprised to see the dials and gauges glowing, the ready lights blinking.

"The nuclear reactor has kept the batteries charged all these years!" whispered Dr. Quest. "A miracle. A tiny bit of fuel will last for centuries."

The captain grinned and muttered something else in German. The pressure gauges spun as the captain opened and closed valves with a practiced hand.

"I hope he knows what he's doing," Dr. Quest said.

"You can't tell?" Jonny asked. He was surprised. He had always thought his father could operate any kind of machine or device.

"Negative," said Dr. Quest. "This old ship is a total mystery to me. We have to play along with him at least until he gets the ship out of the cavern, into the open water."

The captain grinned and muttered a few more words in German.

"Stand by the periscope," Jonny's father whispered. "Just look busy and let him handle everything."

The mad glint in Captain Grimm's eye had turned to lightning. Jonny looked into those eyes and saw an evil far colder than the squid's. For the first time since leaving the surface, he was truly afraid.

The captain shouted, then laughed.

"What's he saying?" Jonny asked his father. The floor was tilting under his feet.

"'Dive!' He's saying, 'Dive!'"

9

ELECTRIC MOTORS WHINED.

Propellers whirred and spun.

Valves opened and switches closed, and the U-232 began to move forward and down, into the water.

The old rivets of the ship creaked and groaned as the ballast chambers filled with water.

The Nazi submarine began to shiver and vibrate as it slipped under the surface of the pool in the cavern.

"It's working!" Jonny said.

"We're moving!" Hadji whispered.

Dr. Quest smiled under his loose-fitting tape gag.

The three of them watched as Captain Grimm, still talking to himself, opened valves and pressed buttons, spun wheels and pulled levers, sending the ancient U-boat deeper and deeper.

The sound of rushing water could be heard from forward and back, as the ballast tanks filled, trimming the submarine for underwater operation.

The whir of the electric motors became a smooth whine. Underwater, the U–232 was in its element.

It was a submarine again.

"How can Captain Grimm see where he's going?" Jonny asked. The only windows in the control room were the portholes on either side. There was nothing facing forward.

Gesturing with his chin, Jonny's father pointed toward a crude TV monitor set into the wall near the ceiling. On the screen crude lines and dots crossed and flashed, like a primitive video game.

"He's using a sonar imaging system," Dr. Quest said. "Hear those pings?"

Jonny listened. Underneath the whine of the electric motors, he could hear a high pitched *PING PING PING*.

"The ship sends out sound waves that bounce off the walls of the cave. The sound waves are used to map the cavern, and the captain steers by the image on the screen."

"Pretty primitive," said Hadji.

"Let's just hope it works," said Dr. Quest.

The submarine turned underwater and began to move down and out of the cave.

Jonny had to grip the handholds along the walls because the deck was tilting so steeply.

Get us out of here! Jonny thought. He could

hardly wait to see the sun and breathe the fresh air. He could hardly wait to see Jessie and Race Bannon.

The propellers thrashed the water as the U–232 dove deeper and deeper, into the tunnel that led to freedom.

"Hooray!" whispered Hadji.

Through the portholes on either side of the control room, Jonny could see the rock walls of the cavern, moving by slowly at first, and then faster and faster.

PING PING PING.

The captain's single eye was fixed on the sonar screen. His wooden leg was planted firmly on the steel deck. His ancient wrinkled hand was on the sub's steering wheel.

Through the porthole, the cave wall sped by faster and faster—and then:

"What's that?" Hadji whispered.

Jonny Quest looked out the other porthole.

He saw the tentacles, lined with saucer-sized suckers, groping, grabbing, slithering through the water toward the submarine.

The water turned dark with silt.

The U–232 shuddered and groaned—and stopped!

The mad captain shouted in German and spun the wheel uselessly.

The deck pitched under Jonny's feet; the chairs began to slide across the floor.

The ship was being dragged backwards!

"Hang on!" Jonny shouted, as Hadji and Dr. Quest were flung like dolls across the control room.

The boat tipped as it was lifted from the water and groaned like a living thing as the ballast tanks emptied.

The light through the porthole told Jonny that the U-boat was back on the surface of the water.

Everything was still.

The captain was muttering in German again, the same phrase over and over.

"What's he saying?" Jonny asked.

"Something about the Demon of the Deep," said Dr. Quest. "Apparently this happens every time he tries to leave. The giant squid pulls him back into the cave. That's why he is still here after fifty years!"

The seas were breaking.

Before, they had been smooth swells, lifting the Quest catamaran up and down, slowly and gently, like the breathing of a great sleeping beast.

Now, the beast had awakened.

Jessie watched the rising wind tear the tops off the waves, hurling them at the catamaran in shreds of water and spray. The seas tore at the sails and the ropes and the railings, sweeping across the decks.

Jessie held onto the mast while she tried to pick up the *Belle of the Deep* on the radio. No luck. She couldn't get Jonny's deepsuit on the locater, either. She knew her friends were down there somewhere! She feared they were in danger! Even though she got nothing but static, she kept trying.

Her father, Race Bannon, was at the stern of the catamaran, trying to coax a little more slack out of the winch. If he could loosen the cable even a little, the catamaran would ride the waves better.

"Woof, woof," said Bandit, as if he were trying on his own to raise Jonny and Hadji and Dr. Quest from the deep.

"I agree," said Jessie. "If we keep trying we'll make contact."

SPLASH!

Jessie ducked her head as a giant wave washed over her. She didn't mind. She was already wet all over.

Then she heard, "woof, woof!" from farther away.

"Bandit!" she cried.

The wave had lifted the little dog into the air and was sweeping him across the deck, toward the side of the catamaran.

"Hold on!" Jessie yelled, "Grab the railing!"

But of course, Bandit had no hands with which to grab. He was swept under the railing and over the side—into the water!

Jessie ran to the railing.

"Wait!" shouted her father. Race Bannon ran to the side and stood at the rail beside her.

Jessie peered down into the dark wildness of the sea. There in the crashing foam and froth, she saw panicked black eyes and a little black nose.

"Bandit!" cried Jessie.

"Throw this!" said her father.

He handed her an orange donut-shaped life preserver attached to a rope.

Jessie threw it is far as she could into the waves.

"Woof! Woof!" Bandit cried. His barks were getting faint. Jessie could see his little paws striking helplessly at the surging waves.

Too short! Jessie pulled the life preserver back in and threw it out again. Could she make it? Bandit was drifting farther and farther away into the storm . . .

"Incredible!" said Hadji.

He stood at the porthole looking out at the giant squid. Dr. Benton Quest stood beside him.

They no longer had to pretend they were taped to their chairs. Captain Grimm had fallen asleep as soon as the squid had dragged the submarine back into the cave. His head was on the metal control room table, and he was snoring loudly.

"Incredible," repeated Dr. Quest.

Jonny was standing behind them. Over their

shoulders, through the porthole, he could see the giant squid, basking on the surface of the water alongside the U–232.

For the first time, he could see the entire squid at once, and it was the scariest and most magnificent thing he had ever seen.

It was at least a hundred feet long. Its ten tentacles were each the size of a telephone pole. They all came from a sleek body twice the size of a bus, that was finned at one end like a rocket ship.

But most incredible of all were the animal's eyes. Even as the three Quest Team members watched, the eyes rose out of the water and stared back at them.

They were the size of basketballs and very black.

They no longer had the malevolent, eerie, evil expression Jonny had noticed when they had pressed up against the Plexiglas *Belle.*

The eyes had a different look now.

They looked almost warm—almost affectionate.

SNNOOOORRRE!

The captain stirred, then went back to sleep, with his head on the table.

"We'd better do something with him," Hadji said. "While we have the chance."

"What?" said Dr. Quest. "Tie him up? Then we don't have even a chance of getting out of here."

"I've got an idea!" said Jonny. "Let's do

something with you. Make him think you're someone else!"

"What?" asked Hadji.

"Come on," said Jonny Quest. "Help me."

With Dr. Quest's help, they dragged two skeletons from the corridor into the control room. Moments later, the skeletons were taped upright in the chairs, wearing the orange-and-black jumpsuits—and Dr. Quest and Hadji were dressed in Nazi sailors' jackets, like Jonny.

"One more throw!" said Jessie.

The life preserver had missed again, and Bandit was drifting farther and farther away.

Jessie threw as hard as she could, into the spray and roaring waves. The wind caught the life preserver and spun it like a Frisbee.

"Do you have him?" asked Race Bannon.

"I can't tell!" Jessie said.

She pulled the rope in hand over hand, but it was impossible to tell if the little dog was holding on or not.

The rope reached the edge of the boat, and she saw the orange life preserver bobbing up and down in the water.

She bent over the side—and there in the center of the "donut," protected against the waves, was a familiar little black nose and two grateful black eyes.

"Woof, woof!" came a soggy bark.

"Bandit!" Jessie said, reaching down to haul the shaking, dripping dog up onto the deck of the catamaran.

"Woof!" said Bandit.

"Woof yourself," said Race Bannon, grinning happily as he clipped a leash onto the tiny shaking dog.

At least one endangered member of the Quest Team had been rescued. Now for the other three!

"Oh!"

Race and Jessie both jumped back out of the way, laughing.

Bandit was shaking himself off, spraying them both with water.

Jessie was so glad to see him that she didn't mind. She was already wet all over, anyway. She took the little dog in her arms, remembering all the times he had sacrificed his comfort and risked his life to save her and Jonny and Hadji.

"Woof," Bandit said happily.

"I agree," said Jessie. "We're going to find them, just like we found you." She looked up to her father. "Aren't we, Dad?"

"We're going to do our best," said Race Bannon. "The wind is dropping. We weathered the storm. Now we just have to wait and hope for the best."

He patted his daughter on the shoulder. "I have a feeling our friends will find their way up soon."

*   *   *

"This video will astonish the world!" said Hadji. He was at the porthole with the videocamera he had taken back from the captain, locked onto the giant squid.

"You bet!" said Jonny. "But where are you storing the image? The cable connection is gone."

"There's a disk inside the camera," said Hadji. "It'll store a full twenty minutes. Enough to prove what we have seen."

"If we get it to the surface," said Dr. Quest.

Captain Grimm was still snoring at the table. He looked as if he might sleep for years.

Jonny looked at his father in dismay. He had been so thrilled by the sight of the giant squid that he had almost forgotten that they were its prisoners, here in this cave far under the sea.

"Here she comes again," said Hadji, his videocam rolling.

The squid rose from the water, raised its huge dripping tentacles, and wrapped them around the U-boat.

Its huge black eye was pressed against the porthole, filling it. Staring inside, as if . . .

As if . . .

"I've got it!" Jonny said.

"Got what?" his father asked.

"What are you talking about?" asked Hadji, who stopped recording. There was nothing to see now anyway, except for the eye. "What have you got?"

"The way out of here," said Jonny. "I know why the squid is keeping us prisoner. I know why she won't let us go!"

"Why?" asked Hadji and Dr. Quest at once. "What is it?"

"Love," said Jonny. "She's in love!"

10

"I DON'T GET IT," SAID HADJI.

"I DON'T GET IT," SAID HADJI.

He had followed Jonny into the rear corridor leading to the sub's radio room. Jonny was pulling the uniform jacket from a skeleton sitting at a dusty vacuum tube radio.

"Sorry, pal," Jonny said. "You won't be needing this jacket, but we will!"

"I don't get it. We already have jackets!" complained Hadji.

"Grab the jacket off that other sailor," said Jonny. "And follow me. You'll see!"

Back in the control room, Jonny draped a jacket over each of the two portholes.

"Now I can't see out!" said Hadji protested.

"More to the point," said Dr. Quest, "the light can't get out. I see what you are doing now, Jonny! Your theory is that the giant squid thinks the porthole is an *eye*."

"Exactly," said Jonny. "If we cover them, she will

no longer mistake the U–232 for another creature. She will lose interest and allow us to go on our way."

"I hope you are right," said Hadji.

"It's at least worth a try," said Dr. Quest.

He woke up the captain by shaking his shoulder and speaking to him in German.

The captain sat up, rubbing his eyes, then rushed to the sub's controls and started throwing switches.

"What did you tell him?" Jonny asked.

"I told him we had intercepted radio signals from American shipping on the surface," Dr. Quest said. "He thinks I'm his first mate. He thinks the war is still going on."

"What's he saying?" asked Hadji.

"Same thing as before," said Dr. Quest, grinning. "Prepare to dive!"

Grimm barked orders in German.

He turned valves and opened switches, and soon the submarine was filled with the now-familiar sounds of rushing water, whining motors, and whirring propellers.

Jonny and Hadji grinned at one another nervously as the U–232 slipped under the surface.

Hadji lifted a corner of the jacket and peered through the porthole.

"She's ignoring us!" he said.

"So far," said Jonny. "Let's hope for the best!"

"It appears that you were right, Jonny," said Dr. Quest. "It was the 'eye' that fascinated the giant squid. Perhaps she mistook us for one of her own kind. Without seeing the light of the porthole, she has no interest in us whatsoever."

"Hooray," said Jonny and Hadji as the submarine dove deeper and picked up speed.

Even the mad captain seemed pleased. He was standing up straighter—and looking younger.

He was finally going to get his freedom. And his war!

PING
PING
PING

. . . went the sonar as the sub sought its way through the winding cavern.

The captain was studying the crude picture on the video screen. He spun the wheel expertly to the left and the right, following the tunnel perfectly, never scraping on the rocky walls.

"If *sonar* is sound," Jonny asked, "how does *sound* make a picture?"

"How does light make a picture?" Dr. Quest said. "Light is just radiation. The picture is made by our brain, which arranges the signals into a pattern we can understand. The sonar works the same way. Did you ever wonder what a bat *sees?*"

"Bats don't see," said Jonny. "They are as blind as, well, as bats."

"They *see* with sound, like the U–232," said Dr. Quest. "They use a different type of radiation; they use sound waves. But when it is processed and put together in the bat's brain, it is very likely a *picture* of the same world we see from visible radiation."

Dr. Quest pointed toward the crude black-and-white picture of the tunnel on the captain's video display.

"Just as the captain *sees* the tunnel here."

"I see," said Hadji, giggling.

"I see!" said Jonny.

They all three laughed, and the captain muttered something in German back over his shoulder.

"What did he say?" Jonny asked.

"He said, 'Shut up!'"

On the surface, all was calm at last.

The sea, that had been ripped by the wind into shreds and flags of foam, was a smooth, gray-green swell once again.

The towering clouds that had been on the southern horizon, were now marching off to the north, taking their lightning and wind with them, to the coast of New Zealand.

The Quest catamaran was rocking gently on the swell. The cable was creaking, but the danger was over.

While Jessie and Bandit watched hopefully, Race Bannon tried the winch. But instead of pulling the cable up, it pulled the stern of the catamaran down into the water.

"Still stuck!" Race said, throwing the winch back out of gear.

"What now?" asked Jessie. "Johnny's been down there for three hours. They must be almost out of air."

"All we can do is wait and hope for the best," said Race. He crossed the deck and ducked into the galley. "Meanwhile, how about some lunch?"

"Woof," said Bandit.

Moments later Jessie and her dad were sitting on the stern, eating bagels with cream cheese. Bandit had finished his dog biscuit and was standing on the bow, tail wagging.

"Wish Hadji and Jonny and Dr. Quest were here to share this," Jessie said.

"Me, too," said Race.

"Woof, woof!" said Bandit.

Jessie looked up from her bagel. She heard a funny noise.

It was a *BEEP BEEP* coming from the control board . . .

*   *   *

The passageway got narrower and narrower as the U-boat threaded its way down from the "bubble" cavern.

Jonny and Hadji watched the tunnel wall from the little corner of the porthole they had uncovered. At each turn the wall seemed closer and closer.

The wall was mostly dark rock and mud, with the occasional flash of a luminous fish hiding in a crack, or the glow of luminescent kelp.

"Is that glowing kelp a new species?" Jonny asked his father.

"Indeed it is," said Dr. Quest. "I think we will find there are many unknown and unusual species growing near the undersea vents. Perhaps they are what attract the giant squid."

"Then we could use the vents to locate giant squid all over the world," Hadji suggested.

"Or vice versa," said Dr. Quest.

"*Achtung!*" said Captain Grimm. "*Heil* Hitler!"

The boys turned away from the porthole, carefully covering it.

The captain was at the wheel of the sub, pulling on a lever. He shouted in German at Dr. Quest, who ran over to help him.

"What's up?" Jonny asked. "More trouble?" He could feel the floor tilting under his feet.

"Not at all," said Dr. Quest, grinning. "We made it out of the cavern. We are in open water at last, heading up, toward the surface!"

"Hooray!" shouted Jonny and Hadji together.

11

JESSIE RAN TO THE CONTROL BOARD. THE RED LIGHT WAS flashing. The radio's locater beeper was showing a *connect* signal.

BEEP

BEEP

BEEP

"I've got them!" she said excitedly. "I'm getting a locater signal!"

"Which radio is it?" Race Bannon asked. "The submersible or Jonny's deepsuit radio?"

Jessie checked the signal. "It's Jonny," she said. "The deepsuit radio."

"See if you can raise him!" Race said.

"Jonny, can you hear me? This is Jessie! Can you hear me? Come in! Come *in!*"

There was no answer.

"Darn!" She banged on the control board with her fist. "According to the locater beeper, he's right below us," she said. "And he's on his way up. But slowly!"

*   *   *

Far below, Hadji and Jonny were holding onto the metal table in the control room of the U-232, trying to keep from falling.

The German submarine was climbing at a steep angle, toward the surface, its electric engines whining.

The pumps wheezed and the servos whirred as the vessel struggled to rise in the open sea.

It's almost like an old dog, Jonny thought. *Too old to run anymore.*

"I want to video the cliff," Hadji said. He raised his videocamera to the porthole and pulled the jacket aside.

"No," Jonny said, putting one hand on his friend's shoulder. "We're not safe yet. We're still in the giant squid's domain. What if she saw the porthole and thought it was an eye, and pulled us back down into the cave?"

"You're right," Hadji said. He covered the porthole again. He smoothed the jacket down, to show Jonny that he understood. "But how come we're rising so slowly?"

Jonny shrugged. He turned and was surprised to see his father at the controls. "You're running the boat, Dad?"

"Captain Grimm thinks I'm the first mate, remember?" said Dr. Quest. "And I know enough

91

from watching him to run the sub in the open water. I'm following the cable up slowly because I'm not sure this old tub can handle sudden pressure changes."

"Where's the nutty Nazi?" Hadji asked.

"He heard a beeping noise in the torpedo room," said Dr. Quest. "He went to check it out. I figure he can't hurt anything because there are no torpedoes left."

Jonny opened the forward door and heard a faint *beep, beep, beep.*

"I hear it, too," he said. "I'd better go check it out."

"Good idea, son."

As he stepped over the skeletons in the corridor, Jonny heard the beeping noise getting louder.

What could it be? he wondered. *Dad said the radio equipment on the sub was all dead, since the vacuum tubes exploded long ago.*

Then he remembered: the deepsuit! It had a locater beeper built into the radio.

I took it off and left it in the torpedo room! That noise must be Jessie, trying to contact us now that we are out of the cave!

Jonny increased his pace to a run. *Now I'll be able to radio Jessie on the surface,* he thought excitedly. *I can tell her and Race—and Bandit!— that the Quest Team is coming home!*

Better than that, in fact, Jonny realized with a smile. They were coming home with the first video of the giant squid, and more—a genuine Nazi submarine from World War II!

As he unsealed the door to the torpedo room, Jonny heard a familiar voice. "Jonny, can you hear me? Come in . . ."

Then there was a burst of static, followed by a loud ripping sound and a cackle of insane laughter.

And then silence.

Jonny flung the door open and saw Captain Grimm holding the radio set ripped from the deepsuit's helmet.

It was ruined!

The mad submariner held up the circuit board and the tiny speaker, grinning triumphantly. Then he rushed past Jonny, out the door, and ran down the corridor toward the control room.

Jonny followed.

The scene in the control room was chaos.

Dr. Quest stood at the wheel. Hadji was backed against a wall, trying to look inconspicuous.

Captain Grimm was waving the ripped-out radio in one hand and the Luger in the other.

He was shouting at the two skeletons that Jonny

and Hadji had dressed in the orange-and-black jumpsuits. He thought they were the American "spies," and he was shouting at them in English.

"I found the secret radio you used to give away our position!" he screamed. "But now your game is ended. The penalty for such treachery is—*death!*"

The insane Nazi put the Luger to the head of each corpse and fired once.

Click!

Click!

Jonny could tell by the triumphant look on the old man's face that he thought the gun had actually fired. He thought he had *killed* the skeletons!

Jonny looked at his father, who shrugged and went back to his work directing the sub up to the surface.

Who cared how crazy the old man was? Soon they would be safe on the surface anyway.

"Lost them!" Jessie said.

She banged on the control board with her fist.

The beeper light was out. The signal was gone.

"Jonny! Jonny!" Jessie tried once more over the speakerphone.

There was no answer.

"What could have happened this time?" she protested. She scanned the dial across every frequency, a desperation move, but she got nothing.

She turned away from the control board in frustration and saw her father, Race Bannon, holding a pair of binoculars.

"I lost the locater signal," she said.

"Let it go for now," said Race. "We have another problem."

"We do?"

Race pointed to the west. On the horizon, Jessie saw a dark mass that looked almost like a mountain.

Except that it was square on top, like a building.

A skyscraper—at sea? "What is that?" she asked.

"A supertanker," her father said. "And it's coming straight at us."

12

"WHAT'S THE NUTTY NAZI MUTTERING ABOUT?" JONNY ASKED.

The U–232 was rising slowly through the Pacific. According to the submarine's depth gauge it was still over 500 feet below the surface.

The German captain, Grimm, was grinning and muttering insanely to himself. He was spinning the ancient Luger around on his finger and holstering it like a cowboy.

"He is talking about war," said Dr. Benton Quest. "War is his religion. He can't wait to sink some ships and watch the Americans drown. He thinks we are his crew, of course. He says we are fortunate to be chosen by the Reich for this historic mission. He says we should be proud to be Nazis, and so forth."

"Yeecch," said Hadji.

"Uggghh," said Jonny.

"We're lucky he's out of torpedoes," said Hadji.

"Yeah," said Jonny. "Otherwise he would probably try to blow the Quest catamaran out of the water."

"He's the one who's lucky," said Dr. Quest. "If I

96

thought he could do any harm, I would lock him in a storage room. But since he's harmless, we might as well let him rant and rave."

"I can't wait to hit the surface and get on board the Quest catamaran," said Hadji. "I haven't had a bagel all day."

Jonny stared at his skinny friend and adopted brother. Hadji Bingh amazed him. He was as thin as a rail, as wiry and agile as a ferret. Hadji claimed that the spiritual practice of yogin made him strong. Jonny thought it also had something to do with his bottomless appetite for bagels.

"How much longer until we see daylight?" asked Hadji.

"Soon," said Dr. Quest.

"Can you find the catamaran with the sonar?" Jonny asked.

"Not really," said Dr. Quest. "The U–232's sonar is pretty crude, and it only works well in the cave, where the echoes are positive. Here in the open ocean it is useless."

"It'll be dark soon. How will we find the catamaran?" Hadji asked.

"By following the cable," said Dr. Quest. "The cable doesn't show up well on the sonar, but I have help." He pointed at a bat-shaped triangle moving slowly on the screen. "This giant ray is easy to track, and it's leading me up the cable."

"That's our friend!" said Jonny and Hadji together.

"We're getting close to the surface," said Dr. Quest. "I should head away from the cable now, so that we don't come up under the catamaran. I'll surface a hundred yards away."

He spun the wheel and the floor tilted as the sub turned slowly.

Suddenly Captain Grimm jumped to his feet and said something in German. He grabbed the periscope and began to polish the eyepiece with the cuff of his uniform. Over his shoulder, he gave orders in German to Dr. Quest.

"What's his problem?" Jonny asked.

"He doesn't want to surface yet," said Dr. Quest. "He wants to check out the scene on the periscope first."

He pulled a handle back and the engines cut down to an idle. The U–232 was coasting silently under the water.

"It's not a bad idea," said Dr. Quest. "We can use the periscope to check out the scene before we come up. We don't want to surface in the middle of a storm."

He hit a button and servos whined as the periscope was raised.

"Can't they see us?" Jessie asked.

She was standing by her father's side at the stern of the Quest catamaran.

They were both watching as the giant supertanker bore down on them. It was still several miles away, but it was coming straight at them.

"The bridge is too far aft," said Race. "They can't see over the bow. These supertankers steer by satellite image, and we're not showing up on their map."

"We'd better move our boat, then!" Jessie said.

"We can't," said Race Bannon. "It would mean cutting the cable. What if Dr. Quest and Jonny and Hadji are counting on it to get them to the surface?"

"Woof, woof," said Bandit.

"Maybe I can reach them on the radio," said Jessie. "It's our only chance!"

She ran to the control board and began sending out a flurry of emergency and distress signals.

"Come in, tanker, come in! You are on a collision course with a small boat! Hello, tanker? . . . Got them!"

Jessie grinned at her father triumphantly.

"Put it on speakerphone," said Race. "Let me talk to them while you and Bandit go forward and set off some flares!"

"Woof, woof," said Bandit.

Jessie ran to the center of the bow and took a flare out of the emergency box.

She snapped off the self-lighting time fuse, and watched the flare shoot into the sky. As she watched it rise and explode like fireworks, she realized it was getting dark.

She looked to the west. The sun had already set. The sky was streaked with pink, and the surface of the sea became darker and darker indigo with each passing minute.

The tanker had turned on its lights. It was only a few miles away—and still heading straight at them. Jessie wondered if her father was having any luck.

Just then, she heard him yell—"Success!"

He was just signing off as she joined him at the control board.

"The ship is the *Petroleum Princess*," Race said, "and it turns out that the captain is an old friend of mine from the Navy."

"So how come he hasn't stopped?" Jessie demanded, pointing at the ship bearing down on them.

"He can't stop," Race said. "He can't even slow down. The supertanker we are looking at is almost a mile long. It takes several miles for it to stop, or turn around."

"So what do we do, cut the cable?" Jessie asked. "Or jump?"

The tanker was getting closer and closer. It had what sailors call "a bone in her teeth"—a moving mountain of white foam pushed up by the bow.

"Neither," said Race Bannon. "We got them on the radio just in time. They have started their turn,

100

and they will miss us by a hundred yards," Race said. "It will be close, but you know what they say—a miss is as good as a mile."

"Woof, woof!" said Bandit.

"In about ten minutes, they will pass by right *there*," said Race. He pointed to a spot a hundred yards west—where a gray tube was just breaking through the ocean's surface.

"What's that?" Jessie asked. "A shark's fin? No, it's metal! It's—"

"*Auf,* periscope," barked Captain Grimm.

The U–232 was floating only a few yards deep, so close to the surface that Jonny could feel it rocking with the waves.

"Almost home!" breathed Hadji.

Dr. Quest stepped aside so that Captain Grimm could look through the periscope.

"Might as well humor him," he whispered. "His career is just about over."

The captain put his one good eye to the lens.

"Aha!"

He clapped his wrinkled hands together, exclaimed something in German, and ran out of the control room, stomping on his wooden leg.

"What was that all about?" Hadji asked.

"He said 'ship,'" said Dr. Quest. He ran to the periscope with a worried look on his face.

He looked through the eyepiece—then straightened, blinked, and looked again.

"It is a ship!" he cried. "A big one! And it's bearing down on us!"

"Can you see our catamaran?" Jonny asked.

"Yes, there it is, about a hundred yards away. I can see Race and Jessie on the deck. The ship's going to miss them."

"Hooray!" said Hadji. "Then let's head over there and join them!"

Dr. Quest hit the throttle.

Nothing happened. The engines were silent.

Just then, the captain came back into the room. He was wiping his hands on an oily rag.

Dr. Quest asked a question in German, and the captain answered, smiling gleefully.

"He has disabled the engines so that we can't move," said Dr. Quest, with a look of horror on his face. "And he has rigged the ship to explode on impact. He has turned the U–232 into a suicide bomb. A nuclear suicide bomb!"

13

THERE WAS A LONG SILENCE. THE ONLY SOUND IN THE control room of the submarine was the low sound of the demented old Nazi captain, chuckling.

"What now?" asked Hadji, finally.

"We are stuck," Dr. Quest said. "We are barely under the water, so shallow that the ship can't pass over us. When it hits, it will blow up everything for miles around—including the catamaran."

"Can't we go deeper?" asked Jonny.

Dr. Quest shook his head. "Without the engines we can't dive or move out of the way. We have only one chance. We can blow the ballast and surface, and hope that the approaching ship sees us in time to stop or turn. We still have ten minutes or so. Surely that will be enough time!"

"And if it isn't?" Jonny asked.

Dr. Quest shrugged. "It's our only chance. Help me turn this ballast wheel! Hadji, pull that lever! We're bringing the U-232 to the surface."

At the table, the mad captain chuckled and spun his Luger on his finger, cowboy-style.

Jessie had never seen anything so huge. The supertanker was ten stories tall and as long as two Empire State buildings, laid end to end.

And it was racing in her direction at almost thirty miles per hour!

The *Petroleum Princess* had managed to turn only a fraction of a degree. But already, Jessie could see that was enough. The tanker would miss the catamaran by a hundred yards. It would pass to the left, over the exact spot where she had seen the strange metal tube rising from the water.

The tube was still there.

Race was studying it through his binoculars.

"It's a periscope!" he said.

"Woof, woof!" cried Bandit.

The dog started running up and down the deck, barking excitedly. He was barking at a dark shape rising out of the water a hundred yards away. It rose slowly and sat unmoving on the surface, riding low in the water.

"A Nazi U-boat!" said Race Bannon. Even without the binoculars, Jessie could see the U–232 on the side of the conning tower. "What in the world is it doing here?"

As if in answer to his question, a door opened

on top of the conning tower, and four figures emerged.

Even in the darkening twilight, Jessie recognized them.

"Jonny! Hadji! Dr. Quest!" she called out. They were safe!

Or were they? Suddenly she remembered the supertanker bearing down on them. Too late for another turn—too late to stop—

"Jump!" she shouted.

She heard the scurrying of paws on the deck. "I didn't mean you!" she called out to Bandit.

Just as he went over the side, into the water!

"Can't they see us?" said Hadji. "Why aren't they stopping?"

"It's hopeless," said Dr. Quest. "When I saw the ship through the periscope, I didn't realize it was a supertanker. It's too big to stop or turn in time. It will hit us in less than five minutes. And the explosion will wipe out everything for miles around!"

Jonny heard a mad cackling sound. The captain was on the bridge, looking through his binoculars.

A hundred yards away, out of the path of the oncoming supertanker, he saw Race and Jessie on the deck of the catamaran. Jessie was waving frantically.

Jonny waved back. How could he let her know

that they were all going to die in a nuclear explosion in less than five minutes—unless—unless . . .

Jonny Quest looked down into the dark water and got an idea. He raced down the ladder inside the conning tower, into the control room, and tore the jackets off the two portholes.

Then he raced back up the ladder. The supertanker was less than a mile away, and bearing down fast.

The mad captain was chortling with glee at the thought of his own impending destruction. Jonny saw with horror that he was eager to die for the glory of the Reich—and to take as many innocent people with him as he could.

Jonny grabbed his father's arm with one hand, and Hadji's with the other.

"Come on!" he said. "Jump!

"If the tanker hits the sub, there will be a nuclear explosion," said Dr. Quest. "There's no use trying to escape it."

"But—!" said Hadji.

"Jump!" Jonny said, to both of them. He pointed to the water. Bandit was dog-paddling toward the sub, towing an orange life preserver with his teeth.

They both jumped and Jonny followed. The last thing he saw before he leaped from the sub into the water was the one-eyed captain, shaking his fist at the approaching supertanker.

Jessie could see that something had changed inside the sub. A round yellow porthole had appeared in the hull. *It's as if it woke up and opened its eye*, she thought.

But Jessie was more concerned with her friends in the conning tower of the sub. Would they escape in time, before the tanker hit?

"They're jumping!" said Race Bannon.

He handed Jessie his binoculars. In the dim twilight she saw Dr. Quest and Hadji hit the water, followed by Jonny, who was carrying the camcorder. Then she watched as they swam away from the crippled sub as fast as possible. Hadji, who she knew couldn't swim, was being towed on a life preserver— by Bandit!

But why had the Quest Team left the old man alone on the bridge?

Fascinated, Jessie watched him in the binoculars, stomping in a circle on his wooden leg, shaking his fist at the huge mass of the *Petroleum Princess* as it bore down on the Nazi submarine.

Jonny and the others in the water were rising on the huge bow wave of the supertanker. All three were holding onto the life preserver now, along with Bandit.

Through the binoculars, Jessie watched the disaster unfold. The ship towered over the submarine, which lay almost awash, its yellow porthole half in and half out of the water. Like a behemoth, the supertanker bore down on the crippled submarine—like a hungry monster about to devour its prey.

Then, as she watched in horror, another behemoth arose from the sea.

In the dim twilight Jessie saw massing, waving tentacles rising from the water. She saw a sleek gray-green body the size of many city buses, and a huge cold black eye. She watched in amazement as the tentacles slithered over the steel hull of the helpless sub, wrapping around the conning tower, pulling it under the water while the tiny captain screamed in impotent rage.

The giant squid wrapped its tentacles around the U-boat in a deadly embrace and pulled it under, just as the bow of the *Petroleum Princess* was about to strike.

Through the waves, Jessie could see the yellow porthole, like an eye, disappearing down into the deep.

Then it was gone.

The supertanker passed over the spot where it had been, as if nothing had happened.

"Did you see that!?!" Jessie shouted to her father excitedly. "The demon of the deep!"

But Race Bannon was already gone from Jessie's side. He was at the bow, throwing a rope to the members of the Quest Team paddling toward the catamaran.

"Wow!" said Jessie as she set down the binoculars and ran to help.

"SLIPPERY WHEN WET," Jessie said in road sign, as she helped her father haul Jonny, Hadji, and Dr. Quest out of the water and onto the deck of the catamaran. She was laughing with pleasure and relief.

Her two teen friends laughed with her. Race Bannon looked puzzled.

Dr. Benton Quest smiled.

"That was one close call!" said Race.

Jonny and Hadji looked at one another, and then at Jonny's dad. "If you only knew!" all three said in unison.

Then everyone backed up laughing as Bandit shook the water off his fur, showering them all.

14

"THERE HE IS AGAIN," SAID JONNY. "I WONDER IF HE'S THE same one."

"I wonder if he knows what a close call we all had," said Hadji.

"I wonder why you two are so convinced everything you see is a *he*," said Jessie scornfully.

The three teens were sitting at the stern of the Quest catamaran, looking down over the side at the giant ray that was shadowing them through the bright blue water.

It was a beautiful warm sunny South Pacific day.

The Quest catamaran was on autopilot, streaking through the sea at twenty knots for New Zealand, where a crowd of scientists and journalists were eagerly awaiting the first videos of the giant squid.

Dr. Quest and Race Bannon came up on deck from the cabin, where they had been on the cellular phone with the United Nations, reporting the incident with the Nazi sub.

"Finished?" Jonny asked.

"Done," said Dr. Benton Quest. "We are recommending that the entrance to the cave be sealed off, so that the sub and its deadly nuclear reactor will remain undisturbed forever. What are you kids watching?"

Dr. Quest leaned over the stern and peered into the water.

"This is the same giant ray we followed up the cable," said Hadji. "I think he—she—it—whatever!—is friendly."

"The giant squid was friendly, too, in a way," said Jonny, laughing.

"Too friendly!" said Jessie, shivering, remembering the scene of the tentacles pulling the sub down to its watery grave.

"Lucky for us that she was friendly," said Dr. Quest. "And that you got the idea of uncovering the porthole to attract her, Jonny."

"We're lucky she got there in time!" said Hadji. "That tanker just missed by inches!"

"All of us are lucky," said Race Bannon. "Including our friend, the ray. The nuclear blast would have wiped out sea life for hundreds of miles around. That's why nuclear testing is such a crime."

"Woof, woof!" said Bandit.

"At least we all got to see the demon of the deep," said Jessie.

111

"I'm afraid we haven't seen the last of him," said Dr. Quest.

"*Him?*" said Jessie, disappointed. "I thought you said the big one was a female."

"I'm not talking about the giant squid," said Dr. Quest. "I'm talking about the insane Nazi, Captain Grimm."

Jonny looked at his father, surprised. "You think he survived?"

"Not him personally. I'm sure he drowned when the sub was pulled under. I mean his spirit—the spirit of human evil, that's the real demon. And that's the demon I'm afraid we will always have with us."

Hadji nodded sagely and went below to get a bagel. Jessie and Bandit followed. Race and Dr. Quest went to check the autopilot.

The ray peeled off, and Jonny waved good-bye as it disappeared.

He stood up and stretched. It felt good to be surrounded by his friends and family. It felt good to breathe the air and squint in the sunshine. It felt good to be alive!

In the distance, like a low bank of clouds, Jonny could see the coast of New Zealand, beckoning the Quest catamaran to land.

This adventure was over. Who knew where the next one would take them?

SCIENTIFIC AFTERWORD

THE DEEP OCEANS ARE MYSTERIOUS, ALIVE, AND DANGEROUS. Though you don't notice it, air constantly exerts pressure on you. You don't usually feel this because you are mostly made of water, which distributes the pressure equally throughout your body. A pressure of "one atmosphere" is the weight of all the air above you—all the way to outer space, where our air thins away to nothing. When you go up a mountain your ears pop to make the lesser outer pressure equal your inside pressure.

Diving into water adds the weight of water above you to the usual air pressure. Water weighs so much more than air, that diving down to 33 feet under the surface adds a full atmosphere of pressure on you. This squeezes the air in your lungs and ears, sometimes painfully. Your ears pop to make the pressure inside you equal the pressure outside. Going another 33 feet down, to 66 feet below, adds another atmosphere. Most people find this is close to their comfort level. Even scuba divers with air tanks do not often go below 99 feet, where the total pressure (of air plus water) is four atmospheres.

This is why going more than a few hundred feet down demands a hard shell around us (like the Quest team's *Belle of the Deep* or Jonny's diving suit) to hold off the mounting pressures. The dangers of such descents are worth it, though, because strange life lurks below the "abyssal zone" where light fades away. This occurs at about 6,500 feet down, in pressures of 200 atmospheres. Water temperatures are only a few degrees above freezing and green plants cannot grow in the utter darkness. Still, there are small, soft fish, worms, and octopuses and squid of all sizes, including the giant squid.

Also called the "devilfish," a giant squid can be 55 feet long—a twenty-foot body plus strong, 35-foot arms like those of an octopus. Weighing a thousand pounds, with a foot-wide eye, the giant squid is the source of many seamen's legends. They attack whales and perhaps ships.

In the utter blackness a mile down, many creatures glow by making their own light—reds, blues, and oranges. Special cells and bacteria living within them make eerie, colored lights, some that flash on and off constantly. We do not know the reasons for this, but these fish are probably communicating with each other. Some lure other creatures to them. The deep-sea angler fish has long filaments with lights dangling on their ends. Small fish mistake the glow for smaller prey and swim right into the angler's enormous mouth. Truly ugly creatures with names like "viperfish" prowl the dark waters in search of prey.

In 1977 a deep-sea vessel operating at extreme depths, plunging to a depth below eight thousand feet, discovered a remarkable new kind of deep-sea life. The vessel visited the cracks where two sliding plates, which make up the earth's crust, collide. In those cracks lava erupts from the sea floor, providing hot water and a soup rich in metals. The exploring craft found strange life-forms huddled around these vents. There were large red worms held upright in white, shell-like tubes. Up to five feet long, their dark red comes from the same oxygen-binding process than colors our blood.

Clustered near the boiling vents were the largest clams ever discovered, some as big as hands. Blind crabs scuttled beneath the craft's lights. Jellyfish moored to the bottom had yellow, floating balls that looked like flowers. Such fascinating new life-forms seem to live wherever the earth's plates collide. The open vents in these areas set lava free. Biologists had not guessed that life could prosper in the cold, dark ocean floor, feeding on energetic compounds from the lava.

So far only a few of these vents have been

explored. Much of the deep sea remains shrouded in mystery waiting for intrepid scientists to reveal its secret wonders—and dangers!

Dr. Gregory Benford, Ph.D.
University of California, Irvine